# Stitch Me Deadly

AUG 2011

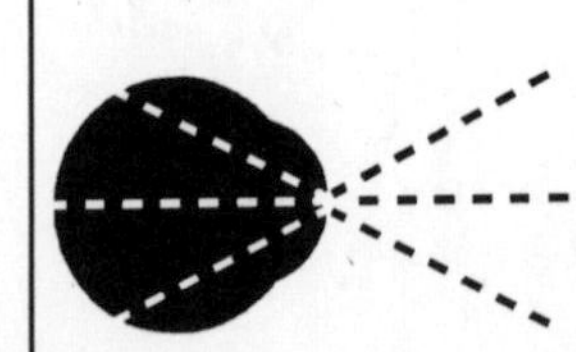

This Large Print Book carries the Seal of Approval of N.A.V.H.

AN EMBROIDERY MYSTERY

# Stitch Me Deadly

Amanda Lee

WHEELER PUBLISHING
*A part of Gale, Cengage Learning*

GALE
CENGAGE Learning™

Detroit • New York • San Francisco • New Haven, Conn • Waterville, Maine • London

Copyright © Penguin Group (USA), Inc. 2011.
Wheeler Publishing, a part of Gale, Cengage Learning.

**ALL RIGHTS RESERVED**
This is a work of fiction. Names, characters, places, and incidents either are the product of the author's imagination or are used fictitiously, and any resemblance to actual persons, living or dead, business establishments, events, or locales is entirely coincidental. The publisher does not have any control over and does not assume any responsibility for author or third-party websites or their content.
Wheeler Publishing Large Print Cozy Mystery.
The text of this Large Print edition is unabridged.
Other aspects of the book may vary from the original edition.
Set in 16 pt. Plantin.

**LIBRARY OF CONGRESS CATALOGING-IN-PUBLICATION DATA**

Lee, Amanda.
Stitch me deadly : an embroidery mystery / by Amanda Lee.
p. cm. — (Wheeler Publishing large print cozy mystery)
ISBN-13: 978-1-4104-3783-9 (softcover)
ISBN-10: 1-4104-3783-3 (softcover)
1. Craft shops—Fiction. 2. Embroidery—Fiction. 3. Murder—Investigation—Fiction. 4. Oregon—Fiction. 5. Large type books. I. Title.
PS3620.R4454S75 2011
813'.6—dc22 2011007851

Published in 2011 by arrangement with NAL Signet, a member of Penguin Group (USA) Inc.

Printed in the United States of America
1 2 3 4 5 6 7 15 14 13 12 11

# Stitch Me Deadly

# Chapter One

I stepped out of MacKenzies' Mochas, the charming brown brick coffee shop and café owned by my best friend, Sadie MacKenzie, and her husband, Blake. I clutched my jacket to me with one hand and my so far unsipped chamomile tea with the other. My throat had been getting scratchy, so I'd taken the opportunity to sprint over — their shop was just down the street from my embroidery specialty shop — at the first break in the rain.

I shivered. Even though it was only sprinkling now, it was a cold rain. But, then, who would expect tropical rain on the Oregon coast in January?

I spotted an elderly woman, dressed in black and carrying a bright yellow umbrella, making her way slowly to my shop, the Seven-Year Stitch. I quickened my step.

"I'm coming!" I called. I reached the door just before she did. As I held it open, I felt relieved that I'd put Angus, my Irish wolfhound, in the bathroom before stepping out. Had he bounded toward me in his usual fashion, this poor diminutive woman might have had a heart attack.

It's rare that, at five foot nothing, I'm able to think of anyone other than a child as diminutive. But this woman was stooped and frail; and perhaps it was due to her black attire, but her skin had a deathly pallor.

"Thank you," she said breathlessly, lowering her umbrella and stepping into the shop. She placed the umbrella in the corner. "May I sit?"

I followed her gaze to the seating area. "Of course."

I took her elbow, fearing she might fall, and guided her to the Seven-Year Stitch sit-and-stitch area. It had two overstuffed navy sofas that faced each other. An oval maple coffee table sat between the sofas on a navy, red, and white braided rug. Red club chairs with matching ottomans completed the cozy square.

I helped the lady sit on one of the chairs. "Are you feeling all right?"

"I'm a bit light-headed is all."

"Would you like some chamomile tea? It might help."

She nodded weakly. "Yes . . . please."

I removed the top and handed her the tea.

Her hand shook as she brought the hot liquid to her lips. She took one sip and then another before lowering the cup and speaking. "Thank you."

"You're welcome. Is there anyone I can call for you?"

She shook her head. "I'll be fine momentarily." She sipped the tea again. "I'm Louisa Ralston, and I'm here to implore you to help me find ivy."

I didn't want it to appear as if I were hovering, so I sat on the edge of the navy sofa to Mrs. Ralston's right. "What sort of ivy?"

She handed me back the tea, and I set it on a coaster on the coffee table. She opened her purse — a quilted black Chanel — and removed something wrapped in layers of white tissue paper. Then with trembling hands, she carefully unwrapped the tissue to reveal an embroidery sampler.

I drew in my breath. It was exquisite . . . and it was old. I'd say it was circa mid- to late 1800s.

"It's gorgeous," I said.

"Thank you, dear. My great-grandmother . . . made it . . . passed it down through the family for . . ." Her breathing became more laborious. "Please . . . help . . . find . . . ivy."

I wasn't exactly sure what she meant, or why she'd come to my shop, but now didn't seem like the time to split hairs. The poor thing really seemed to be in ill health. "Of course, I will, Mrs. Ralston. But, please, won't you let me call someone to come and get you until you're feeling better?"

She leaned forward as if to retrieve her tea and collapsed onto the floor.

I dropped to my knees beside her. "Mrs. Ralston?" I patted her hand. "Can you stand? Maybe I can help you move to this sofa until paramedics arrive."

No response. And her hand was limp. I hurried to the counter, called 911, and explained the situation. The dispatcher instructed me not to try to move Mrs. Ralston and promised that emergency technicians would be there shortly.

I could hear Angus barking and whining in the bathroom, but I knew better than to let him out until after the paramedics had already come and gone. I also knew speaking to him to try to reassure him would only make things worse.

I returned to Mrs. Ralston's side and continued trying to revive her. She was unconscious but breathing, and her pulse revealed a weak, irregular heartbeat.

*Please hurry, EMTs.*

Although it seemed to take forever, the paramedics arrived within ten minutes. Within fifteen, they'd given Mrs. Ralston oxygen, begun monitoring her vital signs, and loaded her into an ambulance en route to the emergency room. I had to hand it to Tallulah Falls' emergency medical service professionals. They were excellent at their jobs.

I opened the bathroom door, and Angus jumped up on his hind legs to give me a hug. When he does that, he's a foot taller than I am. I hugged him and told him what a good boy he was.

He dropped back on all fours, retrieved his chew toy, and trotted into the shop. Before he could discover the open container of chamomile tea and spill it all over my braided rug, I hurried to the sitting area and got the cup and Mrs. Ralston's sampler. I placed the sampler on the counter and went to the bathroom to pour the remainder of the tea down the sink before tossing the cup into the garbage.

I returned to the counter and sat down on a stool. Standing near the cash register was Jill, who's a dead ringer for Marilyn Monroe.

I sighed. "Rough morning, eh, Jill?"

She simply smiled like she didn't have a care in the world. That was because she didn't. She was a mannequin, and she would smile even if the building were burning down around her.

*Maybe I should paint a permanent smile on my face.*

Batman's archvillain, the Joker, sprang to mind.

*Er, maybe not.*

I picked up the phone and called Sadie. After explaining the situation, I asked if she'd mind watching the store and Angus for just a few minutes while I went to the hospital to check on Mrs. Ralston and return her sampler. Sadie said she'd be over as soon as she helped Blake get some tables cleaned up.

As I waited, I studied the sampler. It had the alphabet in Victorian-style letters — both upper- and lowercase — at the top, followed by the numbers one through ten. In the center of the sampler were a primitive house and trees, the kind of artwork you might find on a child's stencil.

The sides were little squares made to look like quilt blocks, and at the bottom was a verse:

His friends were those of his own blood
or those whom he had known the
longest;
his affections, like ivy, were the growth of
time, they implied no aptness in the
object.

I realized I'd love to make a pattern for it and stitch a copy to display in the shop.

I looked around at the pieces currently on display, all of which I'd made myself. The candlewick pillows on the sofas, dolls wearing dresses I'd sewn and embroidered, finished cross-stitch and needlework projects for every holiday and every season. . . . One more sampler couldn't hurt.

Besides, a copy of this sampler would not only be beautiful, but it would also have historical significance. I could put a plaque with the finished piece giving a brief history of embroidery samplers in general and an account of this particular sampler. Maybe Mrs. Ralston would let me do that in memory of her great-grandmother. I planned on asking her when I visited her at the hospital.

I gently folded the sampler back into the tissue paper, taking care because the thread was faded and the cloth was delicate. I realized this beautiful piece of history should be framed and hanging in a museum somewhere. I made a mental note to suggest that to Mrs. Ralston . . . after I asked permission to copy the pattern.

Sadie strode through the door with a tall cup in her hand. "Your tea," she said, pushing back her hood to reveal her dark hair. "Since you gave yours to the sick customer."

I accepted the steaming cup gratefully. "Thank you so much."

"Besides, you'll need it to knock the chill off. The rain is coming down pretty hard again."

"Thanks," I said again. "I'll be back as quickly as I can, Sadie."

"Take your time. Things are slow at the shop this morning. I'll have much more fun over here playing with Angus."

At the sound of his name, Angus dropped his chew toy and loped over to Sadie. She vigorously scratched his head.

"By the way," Sadie said, as I started out the door, "your tea came from the same pot as your customer's. So if you start feeling queasy, call me, would you?"

"Yeah . . . and thanks for that shot of paranoia." I hadn't even thought that the tea could have had anything to do with Mrs. Ralston's collapse.

"Well, hey, I'm just trying to be on the

safe side."

"The 'safe side' would've poured the tea out if there were any concerns about it," I said, "not given it to the 'safe side's' best friend."

"If it makes you feel any better, I tasted yours, and it seems fine. Besides, you did say the old gal was sickly, which was why you gave her your tea in the first place."

"Good point. I'm sure everything is fine . . . with the tea and with Mrs. Ralston."

That statement would come back to haunt me — and to remind me that one was seldom "sure" of anything. Upon my arrival at the Tallulah Falls Medical Center, I learned Mrs. Ralston was dead.

I returned to the Seven-Year Stitch to find Sadie curled up on the navy sofa facing the shop's picture window. She was thumbing through a magazine. Angus was dozing on the rug in front of her. Both started when I opened the door and set the bells above it jingling.

Angus hurried to greet me.

"What's up?" Sadie asked. "You look like you've just seen Casper the Not So Friendly Ghost."

"Mrs. Ralston died."

"What?" Sadie exclaimed. "Why? It wasn't the tea, was it? Please tell me it wasn't the tea."

"It wasn't the tea. Apparently, she had a heart attack."

Sadie had gone back to MacKenzies' Mochas, and I was sitting at the counter studying Mrs. Ralston's sampler again when Riley Kendall entered the shop. Five months pregnant and finally beginning to show, Riley was a bundle of energy. She emanated a maternal glow that only added to her already breathtaking beauty. Despite the rain, she was wearing suede kitten-heel pumps, a geometric-print maternity dress, and a sunny smile. And she was carrying a magazine.

I felt a trickle of dread creep down my spine. She'd found yet another *something* that Baby Kendall simply had to have. I'd already embroidered fourteen bibs, two quilts, and a blanket for this child.

As Riley approached the counter, I held up my hands. "Don't get too close. I'm afraid I might be coming down with a cold."

She recoiled like Béla Lugosi being confronted with a crucifix in *Dracula.* "Okay. I'll put this magazine on the coffee table." She did as she'd said and then sat on the sofa facing me. "It's open to a darling burp cloth. Could you make one like it?"

"I'll take a look at it after you leave and see what I can do," I said. "How are you feeling?"

"Great. But Keith still hovers." She grinned. "Which I love, of course."

"Of course." I laughed. "And your dad? Are you getting letters from him every day?"

She laughed, too. "At least one . . . sometimes two, if he thinks of something else after he's sealed the envelope. And Keith and I visit him once a week."

Riley's father, Norman Patrick, was incarcerated in a minimum-security prison for real estate fraud. I had gotten to know him during the Timothy Enright fiasco.

Riley nodded toward the sampler. "What's that?"

I related the story of Mrs. Ralston's visit and subsequent death earlier this morning.

"That's terrible," Riley said.

"I know. I need to return this sampler, but I guess I should just take it to the funeral home. Surely someone there would deliver it to Mrs. Ralston's family."

Riley furrowed her brow. "Wait. Did you say Ralston? Louisa Ralston?"

"That's right."

"I know her lawyer. His name is Adam

Gray. He went to law school with my dad."

"Do you think he'd be okay with giving the sampler back to Mrs. Ralston's family?"

"I don't think he'd mind at all. I'm guessing he's in charge of the estate, so he'll be meeting with the family regularly over the next few days." She stood. "Give him a call. I'm sure he'll help you out." She jerked her head in the direction of the coffee table. "Take a look at this burp cloth when you get a sec. I'll call you later to see what you think."

"Okay. Be careful in this rain, Riley."

She winked. "I'm used to it. Besides, I'm not sweet enough to melt."

After Riley left, I took the sampler into my office to make a color copy of it. Even though I was planning to call Mr. Gray to see if I could drop the sampler off at his office after work, I still wanted to make a pattern so I could duplicate the sampler and display it here in the shop. I cleaned the copier glass and allowed it to dry before laying the sampler on the surface. I closed the lid and made the copy on eight-and-a-half-by-eleven paper. I removed the sampler from the copier and sat down at the desk with a pen, paper, and a thread chart.

Although I had the colors on the copy, I wanted to try to capture the original hues of the threads as much as possible. I painstakingly searched within color families for the variant that would best correspond to Mrs. Ralston's original. The letters were done in blue . . . not a cornflower or a periwinkle . . . not a Wedgwood blue. . . . This was a blue that fell somewhere between Wedgwood and Colonial blue. I felt triumphant when I found a close enough match.

My eyes were nearly crossing by the time I got to the stitching that made up the verse. As with the rest of the stitches, I tried to determine what the thread had looked like at its most vibrant, before it had been faded by time. This thread was a shade of green . . . not too dark and not too light. I decided to start in the jade family.

I looked up at my white ceiling for a moment to readjust my eyes. When I looked back at the sampler, it appeared that the verse stitching was not as faded as the stitching in the rest of the sampler. I picked the sampler up and turned it over. From the back, it was even more obvious that someone had torn out the sampler's original verse — which had apparently been done in a shade of rose, judging by the scraps of thread that had been run under existing stitches prior to cutting — and replaced it. But why would someone ruin this antique sampler just to change the verse? What was so important about this particular verse?

# Chapter Two

As the rain began coming down harder, I felt a stab of guilt over having left Angus at home today. We have a fenced backyard and a covered porch, so I knew he wouldn't spend the day wet, cold, shivering, and pitiful. He also had plenty of food, water, and toys on the porch. I gave in to a fit of coughing. Who was I kidding? I was the one who was shivering and pitiful today.

Still, I know Angus prefers coming to the shop with me. But since I was on my way to Mrs. Ralston's house to drop the sampler off to her lawyer, I felt it best that Angus stay at home. I'd have loved to stay home with him . . . with a box of tissues, cough drops, throat lozenges, and a vat of chicken soup.

I keyed into my GPS unit the address Mr. Gray had provided me after I'd explained the situation. Mrs. Ralston's home was farther out of town than I'd expected . . .

farther inland. At last the monotone navigator informed me that "after four hundred yards, you have reached your destination."

My destination was a Victorian-style house — white with black shutters and gingerbread trim. There was a black Cadillac in the driveway. I parked my red Jeep beside it, pulled my jacket hood up, and hopped out. I jogged to the door. Before I could ring the doorbell, however, the door was opened by someone who I could only imagine was Mr. Gray — and the name suited him.

A stooped, mousy man with a red bow tie that looked huge on his small frame, he looked too old to have gone to law school with Norman Patrick. Maybe Mr. Gray had gotten a late start. His hair was . . . well . . . gray, and he had cloudy blue eyes and wire-framed glasses. Plus, he was no more than a head taller than me. Between him and poor Mrs. Ralston, I was beginning to feel positively Amazonian.

Mr. Gray extended his hand. "You must be Marcy."

"That's right." I smiled, surprised he had such a firm grip. "I'm glad to meet you, Mr. Gray, though I'm sorry it's under these particular circumstances."

"As am I." He stepped aside. "Won't you

come in?"

I stepped into the home's foyer and nearly gasped. This place was gorgeous . . . like something out of *House Beautiful* or *Architectural Digest.* Or maybe even MTV's *Cribs.*

There was a stairway to my right with white posts, a mahogany banister, and mahogany stairs. A custom-made blue and rose Oriental rug ran down the middle of the stairs.

I pictured myself coming down those stairs wearing the white dress with green trim that Scarlett O'Hara had worn to the Wilkeses' barbecue. As I floated down the stairs to the swelling musical score of *Gone With the Wind,* Todd and Ted would come to stand — one at each banister.

I gave myself a mental shake. *I must have a fever.*

I couldn't see much of the living room behind Mr. Gray, but I could make out an ornate white mantel. An oil painting of a beautiful woman in a midnight blue evening gown hung above the mantel.

Mr. Gray noticed me looking at it. "That's Louisa in her younger days." He stepped into the living room and motioned for me to do likewise. "She was a lovely person . . . outside and inside. I'll miss her."

As I stood beside Mr. Gray, I noticed him

trying to inconspicuously swipe a tear off his sallow cheek. The gesture made me wonder if he and Mrs. Ralston were more than counsel and client. "Had you known Mrs. Ralston long?"

He nodded. "I guess twenty-five years or so . . . thirty, maybe. She was a dear friend."

"I'm sorry for your loss."

Mr. Gray stared at the painting for another moment before turning away. "Thank you, Marcy."

I handed the sampler that I'd rewrapped in Mrs. Ralston's tissue paper to Mr. Gray. "This is the sampler I told you about over the phone."

He sat down on the floral print sofa and carefully unwrapped the layers of tissue paper to expose the sampler. "You say she brought this to your shop yesterday morning?"

"Yes," I said, going to sit near him on the sofa. "She said she wanted me to help her *find ivy.*"

He frowned. "Maybe she intended to restore the piece or something. It is awfully faded."

"Mr. Gray, this sampler was embroidered by Mrs. Ralston's great-grandmother. I wouldn't think she'd have wanted to change it." I waved my hand near the verse. "Although someone *did* change that . . . so I suppose anything is possible. Did this verse have special significance to Mrs. Ralston or some other member of the family?"

He was silent as he read the verse. Then he answered, "Not that I'm aware of." He rewrapped the sampler in the tissue paper and handed it to me. "Why don't you keep this? I believe Louisa would want you to have it."

My heart leaped at the possibility of being able to keep the sampler — which really was a work of art. But I knew how I'd feel if one of my family members' treasured possessions was given to a stranger rather than to me. "I'm honored, Mr. Gray, but I'm sure one of Mrs. Ralston's family members would love to have the sampler."

"You're quite wrong. The Ralston family is sorely lacking in sentimentality. Your taking the piece would likely save it from the trash heap."

"Really?"

Mr. Gray pursed his lips at my horrified expression. "Really. So please, take it. And if you'll wait here while I get it, there's something else I'd like you to have." He crossed the foyer into another portion of the house.

I'd have loved to follow him, and I was

brimming with curiosity about what he would return with. Fortunately, I didn't have to wait long to find out.

When he returned, he was carrying a small lidded sewing box. "I have no idea what's in here," Mr. Gray said, "but Louisa kept it with her almost all the time. Please take it."

"But don't you think —"

"I think it is one less thing for the trash heap or the auction block if you'd be so kind as to take it."

I smiled. "Then I'll gladly take this and the sampler." I gave him a business card from my purse. "But please pass my number along to any of the family members who might want these items back."

"I'll do that, Marcy, if anyone asks about them. Thank you."

"Thank *you,* Mr. Gray." I left the Ralston home with the sampler and the sewing kit. In one way, I felt I'd hit the jackpot, but in another way, I felt terribly sorry for the family if none of them could see the value in either of these items.

Before going to the shop, I stopped by the pharmacy. I bought throat lozenges, honey, chamomile and echinacea tea bags, non-drowsy cold medicine, and tissues. Hopefully, my purchases would get me through the day.

I'd awakened feeling worse this morning than I had yesterday. The tickle in my throat had become a full-blown ache, and my head was stuffy. I almost — mind you, *almost* — wished Mom was still visiting. It would have been nice to have some maternal pampering. But I didn't need the temptation that she'd offered over and over again to "come back home to San Francisco and open your little shop there."

This was my first winter on the Oregon coast, and frankly, I was finding all this rain a little dismal. While winters in San Francisco had had their fair share of rain, there had been also plenty of mild, sunny days. Plus, winters in San Francisco had Mom's cook, Frances, spoiling me with chowders, pasta salads, and cookies. Winters here, so far, consisted of umbrellas, raincoats, and sniffles.

Not that I wouldn't get used to it. And it wasn't that there weren't things to love about Tallulah Falls in the winter. There was the whale watching, of course. And the agate hunters gathering in the early mornings to check out the bedrock. I went myself once and even found a stone large enough to have made into a pendant. Plus, Sadie and Blake had assured me there would be some warm, clear days when Angus and I could play on the beach to our hearts' content.

I opened the shop and went to the back to stash my cold remedies. Almost immediately, the bell above the door signaled that I had a visitor . . . a customer, I hoped. I popped a throat lozenge into my mouth and went out to the counter.

Rajani "Reggie" Singh — the local librarian and an embroiderer extraordinaire — and a woman I'd never met were standing just inside the shop.

"There you are," Reggie said, approaching the counter. She wore a long, light blue tunic with white trim, matching trousers, and a matching scarf. Her short gray hair was covered by a white rain hat and her small round glasses were spattered with rain. She took the glasses off and cleaned them with the tail of her scarf, then returned them to her face. "Marcy, I'd like you to meet Ella Redmond. Ella is the library's new genealogist."

I smiled at Ella, a tall, angular woman dressed completely in black. The color wasn't very complementary to her auburn hair and wan complexion, but overall, she was an attractive woman who appeared to be in her mid- to late forties. "It's nice to meet you, Ella."

I wasn't aware libraries employed genealogists, especially a library as small as the one here in Tallulah Falls. But Reggie was an excellent librarian, and if she felt she needed a genealogist, I'm sure she did.

"Rajani" — Ella glanced at her companion — "or, rather, Reggie, has told me about your embroidery classes, and I'd love to attend one. I'm new in town, and I think it would be a great way to meet people. Plus, I'm really interested in learning some needlework techniques."

"We'll be delighted to have you. Reggie's class meets tomorrow night."

"Okay," Ella said. "I'll be there."

I looked at Reggie. "Did you know Louisa Ralston?"

Reggie frowned. "The name sounds familiar. I'd probably recognize her if I saw her. Why?"

I explained the events of yesterday morning.

"That's odd," Reggie said. "Had she been sick, or did this just strike her suddenly?"

"I don't know," I said. "I totally forgot to ask Mr. Gray if Mrs. Ralston had been sick. He seemed to have been really close to her."

Reggie tapped a forefinger against the counter. "I wonder what was so pressing that she came out in that driving rain yesterday to find — What did you say it was? Ivy?"

"That's what she said." I retrieved the sampler and unwrapped it for them.

"Oh, this is gorgeous," Reggie said.

"It is." Ella frowned slightly. "The verse does mention ivy."

"Right," I said. "I thought she might be looking for that particular shade of green, but the green used in the verse is more of a jade. Don't you think?"

"I do." Reggie studied the sampler intently.

"Here's the other weird thing," I said. "The original verse was torn out and replaced with this one not all that long ago. Why would someone do that?"

"You know," Ella said, "people sometimes incorporate their family trees into embroidery projects. You don't think Ivy could be a person, do you?"

"I hadn't considered that," I said, "but I kind of feel I should look into it. I mean, she wanted to find 'ivy' so badly."

We chatted for a while about some new embroidery projects, a new recipe Reggie was trying on her husband, Manu, tonight, and Ella's move and her new apartment in Tallulah Falls. Then another customer stopped by to pick up a needlepoint pattern book, and Reggie and Ella took that as their cue and went on their way.

After the customer had left, I called Mr. Gray to ask if Mrs. Ralston had a relative named Ivy.

"Not that I'm aware of, dear, but you might check with some of the Ralston family. Were you planning to attend the visitation tomorrow?"

Actually, I hadn't given it any thought. But now I found myself saying, "Yes, Mr. Gray. I'll be there."

Despite the fact that only a few more brave customers battled the rain to visit the shop, the morning passed surprisingly fast. I was sitting at the counter having some tomato soup when Detective Ted Nash came in. Ted and I had become acquainted during the Timothy Enright case. We somehow had progressed from detective-suspect status to friends, and I felt there was some chemistry between us. We could probably be more than friends if I gave Ted any encouragement. But on the one hand, I'd been casually dating Todd Calloway, who owns the craft brewery across the street. And on the other hand, after being left practically at the altar by my fiancé, David, a year ago, I was rather gun-shy on romance.

Like everyone else who had come into the

shop the past two days, Ted parked his umbrella in the corner beside the door. For some reason, this finally drove home to me the necessity of putting an umbrella stand in that corner. I made a mental note to get one as soon as possible.

"Would you like some soup?" I asked.

Ted shook his head. "I'm here off the record."

"And your being here off the record prevents you from having soup?"

"No, it's not. . . . I've already eaten lunch. I'm here because I'm concerned about you."

*Wow. I'd heard about the small-town grapevine, but this was ridiculous.* "It's only a cold. I'll be fine in a day or two."

"I wasn't talking about your cold. I'm talking about Louisa Ralston."

"Oh, I know. Wasn't that terrible? She seemed like a wonderful person. Did you know her?"

Ted closed his eyes and pinched the bridge of his nose between his thumb and forefinger. He gave a big sigh before dropping his hand and opening his eyes. "Later today you are going to be questioned about Mrs. Ralston's death."

"Okay."

"Okay? That's it? Okay?"

I shrugged. "Um . . . yeah. I mean, after

the whole Timothy Enright debacle, answering a few questions about a woman who had a heart attack in my store will be easy. Right?"

Ted stared at me as if he'd never seen me before. Then he said, "Come sit down with me."

Leaving my mug on the counter, I slowly joined Ted on the navy sofa facing the window. "Why are you looking at me that way?" I asked. "She did die of a heart attack, didn't she?"

He ran his hand through his dark hair, which was prematurely streaked with gray. "Technically, yes, Mrs. Ralston suffered a myocardial infarction. But it was caused by a drug used to treat manic depression."

"Mrs. Ralston was manic-depressive?"

"No, Marcy, she wasn't. And that's why the drug — a central nervous system depressant — caused her to suffer a heart attack."

"That's terrible! That means . . . Mrs. Ralston was murdered."

"Precisely."

"And the police want to question me because . . ." I let the question hang there.

"Because Mrs. Ralston ingested the medication shortly before her death. You were the last person to speak with her and . . ."

"And what?" *Although the weight in the pit*

*of my stomach told me even before Ted did.*

He sighed again. "And you gave her a cup of tea."

"So? It hadn't even been opened. The worst thing I could've done to Mrs. Ralston would have been to give her a cold. There's no way the tea did her in. Besides, I had a cup of tea that came from the same pot just after the paramedics left with Mrs. Ralston."

"What did you do with the cup Mrs. Ralston drank from?"

"I threw it away, of course."

"Of course." He rubbed his chin. "All right, here's what you need to do. Since you have nothing to hide, allow the police to search your shop and house."

"Search my house? That's a total invasion of my privacy." I could not believe yet another murder was being linked to me and my shop. Instead of the Seven-Year Stitch, people were going to start calling it Embroidery Shop of the Dead or Little Embroidery Shop of Horrors. Or worse: Closed.

"Still," Ted said, "it keeps them from being suspicious and getting a search warrant."

"Don't they need to have grounds for a search warrant?" I asked. "I only met Mrs. Ralston yesterday. What reason would I possibly have to want to harm her?"

"I don't know, Marcy. I only came here to give you a heads-up and to try to help. Don't shoot the messenger."

"I'm sorry." I got up and started toward the office.

"Where are you going?"

"To get my house key. If anyone is going to search my house, I'd prefer it to be you rather than some stranger."

"I can't," Ted said. "This is not my case."

"Well, Manu, then." Manu Singh, Reggie's husband, was also Tallulah Falls' newly appointed chief of police. "Can't he do it?"

Ted shook his head. "It's in the county, not the town. If it would make you feel better, I can have the chief see if the investigators will allow him to accompany them."

"I'd appreciate that." I went back to the sofa, sat down, and placed my hand on his arm. "Thank you."

He smiled. "You're welcome."

The bell over the shop door jingled, signaling the arrival of Todd Calloway.

"Well, howdy, Wyatt Earp," Todd said to Ted. He tipped an imaginary cowboy hat at me. "Ma'am."

Ted nodded as he stood. "Calloway." He looked down at me. "If you need me for anything, I'm just a phone call away."

"Is that offer open to anybody, Detective?"

Todd asked.

Ted merely shook his head in disgust and left.

Todd sat down beside me on the sofa. "What's with Earp? Here I am, coming to offer you sympathy and maybe a promise of some chicken soup, and now I'm wondering if I might have to help you make bail."

"Well, not yet. But if you have any funds you'd like to donate to that cause, please hang on to them."

Todd laughed, but I didn't.

"What?" he asked, taking my hand. "Are you serious?"

I explained what Ted had told me about Louisa Ralston's heart attack and the tea I'd given her. "Ted advised me to allow the investigators to search the shop and house to prove I have nothing to hide. I'd rather not do that, but I do want this whole mess to be over as soon as possible. Plus, Ted said he'd see if Manu would request to join the investigators." I leaned my head back against the sofa. "What do you think I should do?"

"It's like you said. You don't have anything to hide. And with Manu observing the whole process, I don't think you'd have anything to worry about."

"So you'd allow them to do the search

without having them obtain a warrant?"
"Yeah," he said, "I believe I would."

# Chapter Three

Fortunately — or maybe unfortunately; I wasn't sure which yet — those county investigators didn't drag their feet. They arrived at the Seven-Year Stitch less than an hour after Todd had left. I was glad to see Manu with them.

Manu approached the counter while the two Tallulah County investigators surveyed the shop with their hands on their hips and their thumbs tucked in their belt loops. I felt they were trying to be intimidating and wondered if they resented Manu's presence.

Manu, on the other hand, looked like an affable uncle. He wore jeans and cowboy boots with his uniform shirt. And his brown eyes were warm and friendly. "Hey, Marcy," he said with a smile. "How are you, kiddo?"

I returned his smile, appreciating his reassuring presence. "I'm all right, all things considered."

"These men are with the county sheriff's

department, and they'd like to speak with you about Louisa Ralston."

As if on cue, the investigators removed their thumbs from their belt loops and sauntered to the counter. The lead investigator took a notepad and pen from his jacket pocket.

"Ms. Singer," he said, "I understand you haven't lived in Tallulah Falls very long. Is that correct?"

"I moved here and opened my shop in September, so I've been here about four months."

"And why did you do that?" he asked.

I frowned. "Move here or open a shop?"

"Relocate," Manu said.

"Oh." I grinned. "The accounting world simply became too exciting for me to handle, I guess."

The investigators did not grin back, but Manu nodded slightly.

"Did you have any prior association with Louisa Ralston?" the lead investigator asked.

"No, sir."

"Had she been in your shop prior to the day in question?" the other investigator asked.

"Not that I recall," I said.

"Did you have anything to gain from Louisa Ralston's death?" he asked.

"Certainly not!" This outburst brought on a coughing fit, and I had to excuse myself to get a drink of water.

"Are you able to continue, Ms. Singer?" the lead investigator asked when I returned.

"Yes, thank you. I'm fine. I've just had a bit of a cold the past couple days, and I —"

"Yes, ma'am. Are you familiar with the drug Halumet?"

"No, I'm not."

"Then there is no reason you should have this drug on the premises of your home or business?"

"No."

"You've never been prescribed this drug. No one in your family takes the drug. Is that correct?"

"To my knowledge, it is."

"Once again, Ms. Singer — you're saying there is no reason why we should find Halumet on any of your properties. Is that correct?"

"That's correct." I looked at Manu, and he gave me another slight head gesture. I believed he was trying to convey to me that this was all routine.

"Ms. Singer, we have no search warrant, but we would like your permission to search both your shop and your home for Halumet to absolve you of suspicion in the homicide of Louisa Ralston. Do we have your permission to conduct said searches?" He slid a consent form across the counter to me.

I glanced again at Manu, who gave me an exaggerated blink. I signed the consent form, taking Manu's blink to mean, "Yeah, sure. Go ahead. No big deal."

As soon as Manu and the county police officers left, I called Sadie and filled her in on the search.

"Yikes," she said. "Are you worried?"

"A little," I replied. "The clothes hamper in the bathroom is nearly overflowing. How embarrassing is that? I've been meaning to get the laundry caught up, but I've felt so lousy the past couple days I haven't wanted to do much of anything after I get home."

"You know that's not what I meant. Aren't you afraid they'll find something?"

"Yes, Sadie. My dirty laundry. I don't want Manu and Reggie thinking I'm a slob."

She blew out a long breath. "I'm just glad it isn't my house the investigators are searching. Even if they only went through my medicine cabinet, they'd find prescriptions that expired two years ago."

"If they've expired, aren't they harmless?"

"Maybe," she said. "Hey, I don't have any chicken soup, but maybe I can bring you over a latte and a double-chocolate-chip muffin. Would that help?"

"That would be wonderful. Everybody who comes in tells me I need chicken soup, but I'm thinking there's no cure for what ails a girl like chocolate."

She laughed. "A double-chocolate-chip muffin it is, then. I'll be there in a few minutes."

While I was waiting for Sadie to arrive, I went to the bathroom and dampened a washcloth with the hottest water I could tolerate. I closed my eyes and held the cloth on my face. Afterward, I reapplied my makeup — just the basics — since I didn't want to make it painfully obvious to every customer who came into the store that I had a cold.

I heard the bell over the door jingle and called that I'd be right out. When I stepped back into the store, Sadie was sitting on the navy sofa facing away from the window. She had my muffin and a nonfat vanilla latte with cinnamon waiting for me on the coffee table.

"Thank you," I said, as I sank onto the sofa opposite Sadie and picked up my latte. "This hot coffee will do wonders for my scratchy throat. And the muffin will perk up my woe-is-me spirits." I lifted the latte to my lips, and the scent was almost as wonderful as the taste. The hot liquid both seared and soothed my throat.

"I can't believe you aren't more worried about this police thing," Sadie said. "I'm telling you, I'd be so rattled."

I set the latte back on the coffee table and picked up my muffin. "It's not that big a deal . . . except for the laundry. I'd never even heard of that drug they're looking for."

"Neither have I." She chewed on the inside of her cheek. "But that doesn't mean there's not some of it in my outdated medicine cabinet."

We shared a laugh.

"How are things with you and Blake?" I asked. I knew the trust issues raised during the Timothy Enright investigation had been a strain on the couple.

Sadie sighed. "We're getting there. Blake is terrific, and I love him with all my heart. I'm just still having trouble getting over the fact that he kept things from me."

"And his blurting out to me that the two of you were trying for a baby when you wanted to keep it a secret from everyone didn't help, either." I bit into my muffin.

"No, that didn't help. But it wasn't the big issue. He was right in that if I'd been going to tell anyone, it would have been you.

And I know the things he kept from me were to protect me, but . . ."

"Have you considered counseling?" I asked.

"Yes and no. We discussed it briefly, but we honestly don't have time. Between running the coffee shop and doing everything that has to be done at home . . ." She shrugged. "You know how it is."

"I know, but some things you *make* time for."

"We have been working on our relationship," Sadie said. "We're just trying to do it on our own before seeing a counselor. For instance, we've been doing this thing where we're reading and working out a plan to rebuild our trust."

"Like what? And is this professional advice or tabloid advice?"

"You're nosy when you're sick!" She grinned. "Professional, of course. The most important thing is making the choice that we are going to be open and trusting and focus on our marriage."

"Good. I'm glad. You know I'm here to help in any way I can."

"I know. But things are really going well. We're even having date nights again."

I laughed. "That's more than I can say. Work and this cold have put me on the shelf for a while."

"So you and Todd haven't been out lately?"

"Not in a couple weeks," I said. "He's been swamped at the Brew Crew, and I've been swamped here."

"What about Ted?"

"What about him?" I asked. I knew to tread carefully there. Sadie had handpicked Todd for me, and we'd already had one argument about whether I was interested in Ted. What can I say? I liked both men, but I wasn't ready for a serious relationship with either one.

"Have you and he been out?"

"Nope." I didn't tell Sadie that I thought it was only a matter of time and that if Ted asked me out I'd go. Only by getting to know both him and Todd would I be able to make an informed choice.

Sadie's cell phone rang, and she answered it. She smiled. "I miss you, too. Be there in a few."

"Blake, of course," I said when she ended the call.

She giggled. "Of course."

"I really am glad you two are back on track. I was worried about who'd get custody of me and Angus."

"Me," Sadie said firmly. "But you don't

have to worry about that. I'll call you later to see how that search-and-destroy mission went."

I groaned. "Please don't call it that."

When Manu and the county investigators returned later that evening, I decided Sadie might have made the right call after all. The officer who was apparently the lead investigator placed a clear evidence bag containing a bottle of pills on my counter. The bottle was a tall, skinny brown pharmacy bottle with a childproof cap.

"Can you please explain this, Ms. Singer?"

I looked past the investigator to Manu. He looked as confused as I felt.

"Where did you find this?" I asked. "I've never seen it before. Is it possible a customer dropped it?" I bent closer to the evidence bag and read the name of the person for whom the drug had been prescribed. "Selena Roxanis . . . That name doesn't sound familiar, but there were a lot of people in last week. I suppose —"

"The drugs weren't found in your shop, Ms. Singer. They were found at your house."

I looked from Manu to the lead investigator and back again. "That's not possible."

"It's true," Manu said. "The bottle was in a nightstand in your guest room."

I stared at him blankly, my mind struggling to grasp what was happening.

"Is that the room your mother occupied last week?" Manu asked.

"Yes," I said, "but I don't know why she'd have this woman's medication."

The lead investigator stepped between Manu and me. "Ms. Singer, we need you to come down to our offices and answer some questions."

"I'll drive her," Manu said, "if that's all right."

"That's fine with me, Manu — er, Chief Singh," I said.

The lead investigator nodded brusquely. "We'll meet you there."

He and his partner left the store.

I was trembling so badly I had to give my keys to Manu and have him lock up the shop. It was a good thing I didn't have to drive myself. It was a better thing I wasn't going to the police station in the back of a county squad car.

Manu opened the passenger's side of his cruiser, and I got in and fastened my seat belt.

"Manu, I'm —" I began, but he was already closing the door and moving around to the driver's side of the car.

When Manu got into the car, I finished

my sentence. "I'm innocent. I had nothing to do with Louisa Ralston's death, and I don't know how that stuff got into my nightstand. I didn't even know Mrs. Ralston. And even if I had, I wouldn't have hurt her."

"I believe you," he said. "What about your mother? Does she know a Selena Roxanis?"

"I don't know. I don't know." I took a deep breath and tried to think. "I'm sorry about the laundry. I usually don't let it get so far behind. Oh, what about Angus? I need to call Sadie and have her take care of him."

"Angus will be fine. You need to call your mother."

"That's right. I do." I fumbled in my purse until I found my cell phone. I dialed my mom, but the call went straight to voice mail. I hung up and redialed three more times. No luck. Finally I gave up and left a message:

"Mom, it's me. I'm on my way to jail right now because of some pills that were in the guest room. If you know anything about them, call me immediately. This is not a joke. The pills were prescribed for someone named Selena Roxanis, and they're called Halumet. Please call my cell or call the Tallulah County Sheriff's Department as soon as you get this message. I'm in big trouble, Mom."

I ended the call but didn't put the phone back into my purse. I clutched it as if it were a lifeline.

"Manu, what am I gonna do? Will they believe me? Will they realize I'd never even met Mrs. Ralston before yesterday?"

"Okay, listen to me," Manu said. "We don't have much time. I know you had nothing to do with Louisa Ralston's death. But you don't need to go into that interrogation room blind."

"Am I going to be arrested?"

"No. I'll stay with you."

"Thank you. You don't know how much this means to me," I said. "Do you need to call Reggie and let her know?"

"I'm fine. Please listen to what I'm telling you. I expect them to question you and then let you go."

"Do I need a lawyer?" I asked.

"Not at this point. You didn't touch the prescription bottle at the shop, and you said you hadn't seen it before then."

"I hadn't. I swear."

"I believe you. Once you allow the officers to fingerprint you, your prints will be compared to those on the bottle, and you'll be exonerated."

"But that doesn't prove anything, does it? What if I wore gloves?"

Manu sighed. "Did you wear gloves to open the bottle?"

"No."

"Then please don't say things like that during the interrogation. If you — or anyone else — wore gloves to open the bottle, then there probably aren't any prints on it."

"Oh. That's good, then," I said.

"That's very good."

"Unless Mom stole that bottle from this Selena chick for some reason and then wiped the fingerprints off of it. Maybe *she* was planning to kill someone with it. Selena, I mean. Not Mom."

"Can we please not borrow trouble? I'm trying to help you, Marcy."

"I know. I know. I'm sorry. I'd never seen that bottle until just a few minutes ago. And I've never touched it, so my fingerprints are definitely not on it."

"Good. Now, simply retell your story. The officers will take your prints, see that there's no reason to suspect you in Mrs. Ralston's death, and I'll bring you back to your shop."

"Yeah, but here's the problem, Manu. I told my story back at the shop, and now I'm on my way to jail. Apparently, my story isn't good enough."

"Your story is fine," he said. "It's the truth. The investigators are only trying to shake you up. They're seeing if you change your story or confess to something. Everything will be fine."

I didn't say anything, but I was thinking, *The last time you told me that, I got ordered to come to police headquarters.*

Manu pulled in behind the two officers and parked in the first available visitors' spot. He opened the car door for me, and I got out as the Tallulah County investigators waited on the sidewalk. They looked very tall and very imposing from where I stood.

The two men led Manu and me through a couple sets of locked doors and into an interrogation room. The room had green-and-yellow-plaid industrial carpet that had a coffee — I hoped — stain or two, yellow-green walls, and metal chairs with rust-colored padding. A gray metal table was bolted to the floor in the middle of the room.

I was instructed to sit on one side of the gray table. Manu had to sit in a chair near the door, and the detectives sat opposite me at the table.

"Let's reacquaint ourselves," said the lead investigator, pressing the PLAY button on a tape recorder. "I'm Detective Bailey." He had thinning dark blond hair and a bushy mustache. I got the feeling he was attempting to be friendly, but his demeanor barely rose above civil.

Detective Bailey gestured to his partner. "This, of course, is Detective Ray."

Detective Ray gave me a curt nod. He had thick gunmetal gray hair and brows knit together like two white caterpillars. His demeanor didn't make it above civil. In fact, I'd say it was a little below.

"Now, let's get a fresh start here, Ms. Singer," Detective Bailey said. "You gave us permission to search your business and home, did you not?"

"I did."

"And you were aware that we were searching for a prescription medication called Halumet, were you not?"

I nodded.

"Would you answer the question, please?" he asked.

"Um, yes, I knew what you were looking for."

"And you knew the reason we were searching for the prescription medication Halumet was because it was found to have contributed to the death of Louisa Ralston, a woman who visited your shop just prior to her demise," Detective Bailey said. "Is that correct, Ms. Singer?"

"That's correct."

"We found this bottle of Halumet at your residence." He looked at the bottle. "It has been prescribed for someone named Selena Roxanis. Do you know this person?"

"No, I do not."

"Do you know how this medication came to be at your residence?" Detective Ray asked.

"No. All I know is that my mother stayed in the guest bedroom where the medication was found when she visited a couple weeks ago," I said. "I'm thinking she must have had it with her for some reason."

"Does your mother suffer from any type of illness for which Halumet would be prescribed?"

"Not that I know of."

Detective Ray raised his caterpillar eyebrows. "So then you think she might've been prescribed the medication and failed to mention it to you?"

"I suppose that's possible," I said. "I don't know where that bottle came from. If Chief Singh hadn't been with you, I'd have believed you planted it." I shot a look of triumph in Manu's direction, but he was wincing as if he had a headache or something.

"Are you accusing us of planting evidence?" Detective Bailey asked.

"No. I'm only saying that I've never heard of this Selena Roxanis, and I've never seen her medicine. And even if I had, I would never have used it to hurt anyone — much less an innocent customer I'd just met."

The investigators told me they'd be in touch, instructed another officer to fingerprint me, and reminded me not to leave town.

I was weary to the bone — physically and emotionally — when I finally drove my Jeep into my driveway. I'd had a class tonight but had called everyone and canceled while Manu drove me to the shop from the police station. I told everyone I had a cold — which was true, so I didn't really lie. Technically. I just didn't tell them I wanted to go home and bury my head under the covers because I'd been in a police interrogation room most of the afternoon and was feeling scared and sorry for myself.

As I walked up the sidewalk to the door, I could see from my vantage point Angus jump up and hang his front paws over the back fence at the side of the house.

"Hi, sweetheart," I said. "I'm sorry I'm so late."

He whimpered as he picked up on my deflated tone.

I went to the door, unlocked it, and hurried through the house to let Angus in at the back door. I slumped onto the kitchen floor, and he draped his six-foot, one-hundred-fifty-pound body across my lap. I cuddled him to me, and we stayed that way until the phone rang several minutes later. I started not to answer it, but I was hoping it was Mom. I still hadn't heard back from her, and so I still didn't have proof that I had not brought that bottle of Halumet into my house. Hopefully, my fingerprints' not being on the bottle would clear me of suspicion, but that would take a couple days at best.

The phone rang again, and I slid my petite frame from beneath the lanky gray dog. I got to my feet and answered the phone. I was not disappointed.

"Mom, thank goodness it's you. Did you get my message?"

"Yes. Are you all right? They didn't strip-search you or anything, did they?"

"No, I'm fine. You've worked on too many prison-movie sets."

"Nonetheless, I'm flying out first thing tomorrow so we can get this mess resolved."

"Mom, that isn't necessary. You can simply

type up a statement, have a notary witness your signature, and fax it to the Tallulah County Police Department."

"Nonsense," she said. "By noon tomorrow, I'll be *at* the Tallulah County Police Department demanding to know why they're treating my daughter like a common criminal."

"But what about your production schedule?"

"The assistant costumer can handle it for a few days. I got you into this mess, and now I have to get you out of it."

"Speaking of getting me into this mess," I said, "who exactly is Selena Roxanis, and what were you doing with her medication?"

"It's complicated," she said.

When I didn't say anything, she continued. "Selena Roxanis is a haughty little diva, a starlet wannabe who needs to be taken down a notch or two."

"So you stole her manic depression medication?"

"Like I told you, love, it's complicated. It isn't like I got in her purse and took her pill bottle."

"Then how did you wind up with it, and how did it turn up in the nightstand in my guest room?"

"She came into wardrobe one day throwing a tantrum at me . . . as usual. I told her I had a luncheon appointment, and I picked up my purse to leave. I thought that would spare us both some unpleasantness. But oh, no, she *wanted* unpleasantness!" Mom gave a dramatic pause. "She blocked my way, and when I tried to go around her, we both spilled our purses. I collected my things, and she collected hers."

"I'm listening," I said. "Keep talking."

"Well, I later found that pill bottle in my purse. I'd picked it up by mistake," she said. "I couldn't very well give it back because by the time I noticed it, I was on my way to the airport."

"But how did the bottle find its way to my guest room nightstand?"

"I didn't want to miss my flight, so I went on to the airport. Once there, I called the director and told him about the slipup. He said he'd let Selena know so she could get the prescription refilled. When I got to your house, I put the bottle in the nightstand for safekeeping."

"Why didn't you throw it away?" I asked.

"Because I didn't want to run the risk of someone finding it," she said. "Even though I don't care for the little snot, I value my clients' — and their casts' — privacy. I wouldn't dare run the risk of someone selling that juicy piece of information to the tabloids."

"I guess you have a point. It might ruin her career if it got out that she was taking medication for a manic-depressive disorder."

"Or the publicity could make her career skyrocket. Either way, I don't want to be responsible. And, I promise you, Marcella, I'll straighten this mess out first thing tomorrow."

"Wait. You said you put the pills in the nightstand. Why didn't you pack them back up to return to Selena Roxanis when you returned?" I asked.

"Because I forgot about them. Besides, I knew she was bound to have replaced them by then."

"Maybe not, Mom. Doctors don't just replace prescription medications upon request."

"They do for some people, love. Besides, learning a lesson in responsibility and discretion wouldn't hurt her one bit."

"Maybe not," I said, "but it might wind up hurting me."

# CHAPTER FOUR

After speaking with Mom, I felt drained. While I certainly had no motive to kill Louisa Ralston, I had the means and the weapon of choice. Who would believe I didn't know those pills were in the nightstand? If I was on the other side of this investigation, I wouldn't find my story plausible.

I curled up in my white suede chair and pulled my portable embroidery cart closer. The cart is wonderful. In the skinny top drawer it has a selection of threads, needles, scissors, and needle-minders. The two bottom drawers are larger, and they contain fabric, hoops and frames, pattern books, and projects in progress.

The current projects in progress included a christening gown for Riley's baby, the burp cloth she'd picked out yesterday, and a small *Boulevard of Broken Dreams* cross-stitch picture I was making Mom for her birthday in a few weeks. *Boulevard of Broken*

*Dreams* is a painting by Gottfried Helnwein depicting Marilyn Monroe, Humphrey Bogart, Elvis Presley, and James Dean in an otherwise empty diner. Mom was totally going to love it.

This evening I chose to work on Baby Kendall's christening gown. The gown had an intricate ecru-on-white Hardanger border. It was time-consuming, but it was coming together so beautifully that I could hardly wait to see the finished product.

Angus, with his rawhide chew, came to lie at my feet. He understood I was in no mood to play and that I needed to sit still and quietly, peacefully stitch. He seemed content to lie there in a show of support.

I heard the rain pattering outside. While it added to the serenity of the moment, I hoped the weather would clear up tomorrow for Mrs. Ralston's visitation and funeral service.

When I got too tired to work on the gown any longer, I placed it back inside the rolling cart. I stood, stretched, and noticed Mrs. Ralston's sewing kit on the hall table. I got the small wooden box and carefully opened it. The lid was hinged, and although Mr. Gray had said Mrs. Ralston usually kept the sewing kit by her side, the hinges were stiff, as if the lid hadn't been opened lately.

There was a linen handkerchief with a lace border lying on top of Mrs. Ralston's sewing notions. I picked up the handkerchief and unfolded it. It had an *L* monogrammed in the right-hand corner. The monogram was pink, and there was a sprig of ivy encircling the letter.

Mrs. Ralston really liked ivy. Maybe Ella was mistaken in her theory that Ivy was a person. Maybe Louisa Ralston simply had a love for the plant itself. Though what she'd thought I could do to help her find more of it was kind of unclear.

With the handkerchief out of the way, I could see a delicate gold chain at the bottom of the box. I reached for the chain and saw that it held a pendant. The pendant was in the shape of a book, and upon closer inspection I saw that it was a locket. I opened it. On the left side was a photo of a young Louisa Ralston. On the right side was a photo of a baby. Even though the photos were in black-and-white, I could tell the baby was a girl because there was a tiny bow in her peach-fuzzy hair. She was so cute with her chubby little baby cheeks! She had to have been Mrs. Ralston's daughter.

I had to go to Mrs. Ralston's visitation tomorrow evening and talk with her family. If nothing else, I was sure her daughter would want this locket back. I know I would if I were in her place. I put the locket and handkerchief back into the sewing box and closed the lid.

I kept looking at the clock. I was trying to be inconspicuous, since there were customers in the shop, but Mom's flight was due to arrive in less than an hour. Although she'd said she would take a cab to the shop, I felt I should be there to meet her . . . partly because she was my mother and deserved to have her loving daughter waiting for her in the airport terminal, and partly because I didn't know what she might do, and so I felt an almost panic-inducing need to keep an eye on her. Still, I smiled and chatted and rang up threads, canvases, and patterns as if I didn't have a care in the world.

The last — for the moment — customer departed with her periwinkle "Seven-Year Stitch" bag. She gave me a cheery wave before pulling her coat more tightly about her throat with her free hand and hastening on down the street in the direction of MacKenzies' Mochas.

Angus looked up at me and sighed. He'd napped most of the morning. I think my melancholy mood was having an adverse effect on him.

"It's okay, Mr. O'Ruff," I said, prompting him to stand and wander over to the stool behind the counter, where I sat. "This will work itself out somehow."

He whimpered and placed his head on my thigh.

"It will," I said more confidently, lovingly stroking his head.

I spotted Todd outside on the sidewalk. He was heading our way. I smiled. "Todd will cheer us up," I told Angus.

Todd came in smiling as if it were the greatest day ever. Of course, he didn't have the police keeping tabs on him while they investigated a murder.

"Hey, there, bright eyes," he said. "If that smile was as bright as your eyes, Angus and I would have our own personal ray of sunshine to fill up this shop. So why isn't it?"

"Aren't you forgetting something?" I asked as Angus trotted over to greet Todd. "Like the cloud of suspicion hanging directly above my head?"

"I'm not forgetting it," he said. "I'm simply not succumbing to it. Are you?"

"I'm trying not to . . . but it's hard. Of course, Mom is flying in today, and she can provide the police with a plausible — for

Mom, anyway — explanation about the pills they found in the nightstand in my guest room."

He followed my gaze to the clock. "What time is her flight scheduled to arrive?"

"In about thirty minutes."

"Do you need to pick her up?"

I lifted one shoulder. "I should . . . but I really hate to lock up the store. Business has been super today, and I wouldn't want to inconvenience anyone who's come to town specifically for my dazzling array of embroidery supplies," I said with a wink. Although, I admit, all the colorful flosses and threads were pretty dazzling.

"Go on and pick up your mom. I'll mind the store."

"You?" I giggled.

"Do you doubt me?" He placed a hand over his heart in mock anguish. "Granted, I don't know much about embroidery, but I can run a cash register and make change. I figure your customers know pretty much what they're looking for."

"That's true," I said, "but what about the Brew Crew?"

"The assistant manager will keep things running smoothly until I get back . . . probably more smoothly than I could. Besides, I need to score a few brownie points with your mom."

I smiled. Mom had been careful to avoid revealing her opinions on Todd, Ted Nash, or even Tallulah Falls in general during her last visit. The only things she'd really appeared to be pleased with were the shop and the house. And she did mention that if I should decide to pull up stakes, she'd help me re-create both of those things "at home" in San Francisco.

Like Mom, I didn't always like to tip my hand. So I answered Todd with, "You can never have too many brownie points, I guess. Besides, I'm really scared Mom will do something stupid and wind up getting *herself* in trouble."

With that, I grabbed my coat, gloves, and umbrella, kissed Todd's cheek, and rushed out the door. Too bad for me, though. When I got to the airport, I learned that Mom's flight had arrived early, but she was nowhere in sight.

Frantic, I called her cell phone.

"Beverly Singer," she said in such a chirpy, trilling, singsong voice that, given the circumstances, it made me want to scream.

"Mom, where are you? I'm here at the airport, and I was told your flight arrived early and —"

"I'm in a cab on my way to the Tallulah

County Police Department to set the record straight."

I huffed. "I'll be right there. Please don't talk to anyone until I get there." Yeah, I knew I was wasting my breath, but I figured I'd give it a shot anyway.

As I strode back to the airport parking lot, I called the shop.

"Hey, there! Thank you for calling the Seven-Year Stitch, where we have the finest in . . . embroidery . . . stuff. What can I help you with?"

"Todd, it's me."

"Great. So how'd I do? I've been trying to come up with a catchy slogan, but you haven't given me very much time. That's the best I could do off the cuff. I'll work on it."

"Um . . . no, it's . . . it's great." Telling him there was no need for a slogan was rather pointless given the Brew Crew's greeting: *Hi, this is the Brew Crew, home of custom-designed beer. If you can think it, we'll help you drink it. What'll it be?*

I shook off the thought and explained my situation as I climbed into the Jeep. "I'm truly sorry about this, and I'll be there as quickly as I can."

"No problem," Todd said. "Take as long as you need. It'll give Angus and me more time to hone that slogan."

I really needed to get back to the shop as quickly as possible.

As I pulled up to the Tallulah County Police Department, I saw a cab sitting out front. I held my breath in anticipation but was disappointed when I parked beside the cab and saw that only the driver was inside.

I hopped out and hurried to the driver's-side window. "The woman you're waiting on," I began, "is her luggage in your trunk?"

He nodded.

I noticed the meter was still running. "I'm her daughter. If you'll help me get her luggage out of the trunk, I'll pay your fare and you can go on about your day."

He rolled his eyes but agreed, then got out of the car and walked around to the back. He slipped the key into the lock and opened the trunk. He appeared to be moving in slow motion.

"Please," I said, "I'm in a bit of a hurry."

He looked annoyed but sped things up a nanosecond. He took Mom's three Louis Vuitton monogrammed canvas suitcases and set them on the pavement. He then announced his fee and started toward the front of the car.

"Would you mind helping me put these in my Jeep?" I asked.

"Thought you were in a hurry."

"Please," I said.

He shrugged and slowly picked up two of the bags. I got the other one and managed to wrestle it over to the Jeep. The cabdriver didn't seem to be having a problem toting his bags, but mine seemed to weigh a ton. If not for stringent airport security, I'd have wondered if Mom might've smuggled the unconscious body of Selena Roxanis to Tallulah Falls to make the woman confirm that she'd spilled her purse in the wardrobe room.

The driver put all three bags into the back of my Jeep, then strolled back to his car and announced his new fee. I paid it and gave him a small tip. He nodded and drove away.

I took a deep breath and hurried into the police station.

A deputy-secretary sat behind bulletproof glass and spoke to me through a microphone. "How may I assist you?"

"I'm looking for my mother," I said. When I realized how childish that made me sound, I smiled. The woman behind the glass did not.

Since there were no chairs in the stark hallway, I decided there must be a waiting room somewhere and that this gatekeeper had to know where my mother was — well

— *waiting.* The last time I was here, I'd been given the VIP — very improper person — treatment and ushered right on into the interrogation room.

I dropped the smile and tried again. "I'm Marcy Singer. My mother, Beverly Singer, has important information in the Louisa Ralston investigation, and I was supposed to meet her here. Has she arrived?"

"One moment." The deputy-secretary turned off the microphone so I couldn't hear what she was saying into her intercom. After her brief exchange with whomever, she turned the microphone back on to tell me she'd "buzz" me in.

Sure enough, there was a buzz, and then I could hear the tumblers in the lock click. I opened the door and stepped into the adjoining room.

Deputy-Secretary Fife — not her real name, but she had a pervasive air of Barney Fife about her — was there to greet me. She had a metal detecting wand.

"Raise your arms, please."

I complied. When Ms. Fife was satisfied that I carried no weapons or contraband, she buzzed me through another door, where Detective Bailey awaited me.

"Hello, there, Ms. Singer. Nice to see you again. Detective Ray and I have just started taking your mother's statement. You can join us, but you may not speak during our interrogation unless directly questioned by Detective Ray or myself. Otherwise, you will be escorted from the premises. Are we clear on that?"

"Yes, sir." If I wasn't going to be allowed to speak during the interrogation, how could I keep Mom from doing or saying something stupid? Something that might get one or both of us thrown in jail?

"Very well. Follow me."

Detective Bailey led me down the now familiar hallway containing the framed photographs of groups of officers from days gone by. He stopped at the door of the same interrogation room where I'd been questioned. Was this the only one they had? And did they all look alike? Wonder what Detective Bailey would say if I asked if Mom could be questioned in the executive suite? Could he lock me up for contempt? Or could only a judge do that?

Detective Bailey reminded me not to speak until I was spoken to and allowed me to go into the room in front of him. He nodded toward the only empty chair — the one Manu had occupied near the door. I sat on it.

I gave Mom a searching look, but she

barely glanced at me. Her expression was as enigmatic as that of the *Mona Lisa.*

"Let's continue," Detective Bailey said with a nod at his partner.

"Ms. Singer," Detective Ray began in a gravelly voice. Then, with a pointed look at me, he corrected, "Ms. *Beverly* Singer."

*I know,* I thought. *I'm keeping my mouth shut.*

"How did you come to be in possession of a bottle of pills belonging to" — he flipped through pages of notes — "Selena Roxanis?"

Mom reiterated the story she'd already told me, but this time she added, "Had I discovered them before I was en route to the airport, I'd have given them back to her discreetly before anyone hanging around the studio could make tabloid fodder out of the discovery. However, I did call the director and alert him to the situation. When I came across the pills later at my daughter's house, I put them in the nightstand with the intention of packing them up and returning them when I got back to work."

"Did your daughter know the pills were in the nightstand?" Detective Bailey asked.

"No. I didn't mention the incident to her."

"Why not?" Detective Ray asked.

"Frankly, Detective Ray, I saw no reason

for doing so."

"Why didn't you overnight the pills to Ms. Roxanis?" he asked.

Mom pursed her lips as she looked at him, and I silently prayed she wouldn't say anything stupid.

"Ms. Roxanis is not especially kind to me. She basically tolerates my presence. That doesn't sit well with a professional who is as good at her job as I am."

I literally bit down on my lower lip to keep from telling her to be quiet. I considered having a coughing fit or pretending to faint.

She continued. "I hoped doing Ms. Roxanis such a huge favor as protecting her secret — and having her *know* it was I who'd protected her secret — would garner some respect from her."

"Did it?" Detective Ray asked.

"No. As I told you, I forgot I had them and didn't see her again until I'd returned to San Francisco. By that time, she'd already refilled her prescription, and I never mentioned her losing the other bottle in the wardrobe room."

"Thank you," Detective Bailey said. "If we need anything further from you, we'll be in touch."

"I'll be staying with my daughter for a few days should you need to speak with me again," Mom said. "My testimony certainly absolves Marcella from any suspicion in this poor woman's death, does it not?"

"You've explained how the drug came to be in your daughter's possession," Detective Bailey said, "but you haven't given us sufficient proof that she was unaware of its presence in her home or that she didn't use some of the pills on the deceased."

Mom's eyes narrowed, and I closed mine.

"My word should be sufficient proof, Detective," she said. "I give you my word it's true, and I'd swear to it under oath — and I have to tell you my word has never been in dispute before."

"It isn't now, Ms. Singer," Detective Bailey said, "but you can't testify that your daughter didn't find the pills after you'd left Oregon."

"How many pills are in that bottle?" Mom asked.

"How many were in it when it came to be in your possession?" Detective Bailey asked.

"I didn't count them," she said, "but you can be sure I'll find out. And when I do, you're going to put it in writing that my daughter had nothing to do with this Ralston woman's death, and you're going to apologize to both of us."

"Very well, Ms. Singer," said Detective

Bailey, "but for now, you are both free to go."

I continued to remain silent until Mom and I were in the Jeep.

"Are you out of your mind?" I asked as I started the engine. "Were you *trying* to antagonize them?"

"No," she said, "but neither was I going to be intimidated by them."

My right temple was beginning to throb, so I massaged it with my thumb before backing out of the parking spot. "You've read way too many movie scripts, Mom. And when you're angry, you talk like one."

# Chapter Five

Mom insisted on coming with me to the needlepoint class that evening. Afterward, we were going to Mrs. Ralston's visitation, which meant I was going to have to cut the class a few minutes short. I was sure everyone would understand.

Mom had met everyone when she'd visited previously, so introductions weren't necessary. I noticed some of the women looking speculative, as if they were wondering why Mom was back so soon, but given my current situation, maybe they simply thought she was here for moral support.

Vera Langhorne was in attendance. She'd done so well in a previous cross-stitch class that she was out to master as many needlecraft techniques as possible. Frankly, I was glad she was giving needlepoint a go because her cross-stitch project had been a little too difficult and I'd wound up "helping" a bit more than I'd intended. Translation: I pulled out and redid so many stitches, the piece was more like a collaboration than a solo effort on Vera's part.

Still, I liked Vera. She was fun, and she certainly knew how to liven up a class.

Reggie was in this class, too. She was a pro at *chikankari,* an Indian white-on-white embroidery technique, and she, too, had taken the cross-stitch class. Reggie was a gifted stitcher. With her husband being so recently named Tallulah Falls' chief of police, I think she used the classes mainly as a social gathering when her husband was working evenings.

I was happy to see that Reggie's friend and coworker Ella Redmond had decided to join the needlepoint class. The group had eagerly welcomed her. In a small town like Tallulah Falls, it was always nice to have fresh meat — I mean, new friends.

I was even able to talk Sadie into taking the class. I convinced her that needlepoint was easier and faster than cross-stitch, and she was reluctantly giving it a go. Though she and Blake now had their relationship firmly on the mend, stitching gave her a girls' night out-let I think she still needed. It had to be tough both living with and working with her husband, especially while there had been tension between them. Even now, it had to be nice for her to take a break a couple nights a week.

I noticed Mom was talking with Ella Redmond. "The last time I was here," Mom said, "I noticed a lovely Queen Anne Victorian house. Where was that, Marcy?"

"You mean the one in Newport?" I asked.

"Oh, I know that house," Ella said. "It's the Burrows House Museum. It was built for a couple of newlyweds who married when both were in their sixties. It dates back to eighteen ninety-five."

"What a gorgeous place for them to share their golden years," Mom said. "Did either of them have children?"

"I don't know," Ella said. "They divorced shortly after the house was built. Everything went to the wife, and she sold it to another couple, who turned it into a funeral parlor."

"Ewww," I said. "That's kind of creepy."

Reggie laughed. "Not necessarily. You have to have funeral parlors."

"But did the people *live* there while the house was also serving as a funeral parlor?" I asked.

"Probably," Ella said. "After all, there was enough room."

I shuddered, images of zombies flooding my mind.

"You know," said Vera, "the Ralston house

has a similar history. I happened to think of it after seeing Mrs. Ralston's obituary in the newspaper. That house was once a home for unwed mothers."

"Really?" I asked. "It's a gorgeous place. Were the mothers allowed to live there with their children?"

Vera inclined her head. "I think it was more of a case of the women having their babies there and then putting them up for adoption."

"Oh." I bit my lower lip. "That's sad."

"Yeah. Mrs. Ralston and her husband bought the house when they were first married," Vera said. "I remember her telling my mother that she wanted to fill the house with happy memories."

"If the children were adopted into happy families," Reggie said, "then there *were* happy memories there."

Vera shrugged. "Just repeating what I heard."

"And you have to believe," Sadie said, "if there were that many children being given away, there was a great deal of sadness in the place. Too many brokenhearted mothers."

I tried to lighten the mood by asking, "How's everyone doing on their projects? Anyone need any help?" But the mood was somber throughout the rest of our class.

After class, Mom and I went back to my house to freshen up and change clothes before going to the visitation. She wore a dove gray suit and I wore a black shift. Since the shift was too restricting for me to climb into the Jeep, and since Mom flatly refused to be seen "flinging" herself out of the Jeep with her skirt hiked up to her thighs, we called a cab to take us to the funeral home. Life would have been simpler had Mom rented a car, but she preferred to be chauffeured.

When we arrived at the funeral home, Mom asked the driver to "get our doors, please." He did so, and she gave him a whopping tip. She has the regality thing down pat.

We hurried inside out of the cold wind. Mom immediately took out her compact and checked her makeup, then snapped the compact shut and dropped it back into her purse. We were greeted by a funeral home director, who told us where to find the Ralston family. We made our way to the proper room, and I noticed Adam Gray standing just inside the door. He looked even smaller than he had the first time I'd seen him. His black suit hung on his slight frame and made him appear wan and hollow-eyed.

"Hello, Mr. Gray," I said.

He smiled. "Thank you for coming, Ms. Singer."

"This is my mother, Beverly Singer. She's visiting from San Francisco."

"Pleasure to meet you," he said. "I love San Francisco, though I haven't had the opportunity to visit in years."

"It's a pleasure to meet you, too, Mr. Gray," Mom said. "And you'll have to look me up when you do get back to San Francisco."

"I'll do that." He glanced around the room. "Louisa was a wonderful person. She deserved . . . more."

I followed his gaze and saw the sparse crowd, most of whom appeared bored. "I wish I could've known her better."

"I wish you could have, too," Mr. Gray said. "I think you and she would've been friends."

I thought of asking Mr. Gray if he knew of anyone associated with Mrs. Ralston who took the drug Halumet, but I decided this probably wasn't the right time or place.

A tall, thin man in a navy suit, pale blue shirt, and white-and-blue ascot strode toward us. His black hair was combed over to the right and so rigid I wondered if it would move even if I put both hands in it and tried to mess it up. "Gray," the man said with a bob of his head at Mr. Gray. "Who are your charming companions?"

"Carrington Ellis, meet Marcy and Beverly Singer," Mr. Gray said. "Marcy, Beverly, this is Carrington. He is Louisa's sister's son."

"Cary, please," the man said, giving a slight chivalrous bow. "I'm enchanted to meet you both. Did you know my aunt well?"

"I'm afraid not," I said. "She . . . I was . . . with her when she . . . when she . . . became ill."

"Ah, you own the embroidery shop," he said. "The Seven-Year Stitch, isn't it?"

"That's right."

"Charming. I'll have to come in and check it out." He smiled. "I've been searching for an outlet to relieve my stress. Perhaps some sort of needlecraft is what I need."

I wondered if that was true, or if he was an old playboy wannabe simply looking for a new venue to meet women.

"Indeed," Mr. Gray said drily.

I was getting the impression Mr. Gray didn't have a lot of affection for Cary. But, as he was the first family member I'd met, I asked him if he would be interested in the sampler, the sewing kit, or the locket I'd found inside.

"Not me, but thank you for asking," Cary said.

"I told you when I gave you those things that you'd be keeping them from the auction block, Ms. Singer," said Mr. Gray. "Apparently, you didn't believe me."

"He's quite right," Cary said. "Eleanor has already contacted an auction house. She's planning to sell off everything."

"Everything?" I asked.

"Everything that was left to her . . . which is probably the bulk of the estate. Eleanor was Aunt Louisa's only grandchild."

"Are Eleanor's parents still living?" Mom asked.

"Her mother is living, but her father — Louisa's son — died several years ago," Cary said.

"I'm sorry to hear that," Mom said.

I looked toward the people standing closer to the closed casket. "Which one is Eleanor? I'd like to speak with her."

Cary offered his arm, a gesture I thought was outdated for someone his age. He couldn't be more than fifty, yet he conducted himself like a gentleman *from* the 1950s. Still, not wanting to offend him, I placed my hand in the crook of his arm and allowed him to escort me to his cousin.

Mom elected to remain behind, and Mr. Gray seemed happy to keep her company.

Eleanor bore no resemblance to her dainty grandmother whatsoever. She was at least five nine and had a sturdy, muscular build. She wore her chestnut hair pulled away from her face, and other than some bronze lip gloss, she wore no makeup.

"Eleanor," Cary said, "this is Marcy Singer. She owns the Seven-Year Stitch."

"I'm terribly sorry for your loss," I said. "Your grandmother struck me as a delightful person."

Eleanor nodded. "She was dear to all of us."

"I'm sure you're aware she was in my shop when she became ill," I said.

"Yes, well, no one is accusing you of anything, Ms. Singer."

I could've told her otherwise, but I didn't. "She left an embroidery sampler at the shop, and I thought you might want it back."

"I'm not one for embroidery, Ms. Singer. I leave that sort of thing to ladies of leisure."

"But it's very old," I said. "Her great-grandmother made it. Your great-great-grandmother, I think that would be, right?" *Hello? Don't you want this piece of your history, for goodness' sake?*

"Fascinating," Cary said.

"Is it worth anything?" Eleanor asked.

"Monetarily, I doubt it. The original work has been altered. But the sentimental value —"

"Sentiment is something else best left to ladies of leisure," Eleanor interrupted. "Feel free to keep the . . . sampler, did you call it?"

"Yes. Little girls used to make embroidery samplers to review their alphabet and verses while learning to make various stitches," I said.

"Well," Eleanor said, "do whatever you'd like with it."

"If you're sure you don't want it, I'd love to frame it and display it in the shop with a history of samplers and a bit of information about Mrs. Ralston and her great-grandmother."

"That'd be nice." She looked up at her cousin. "Will you take care of getting whatever information Ms. Singer needs?"

"Of course," Cary said.

"If you'll excuse me," Eleanor said, "I need to speak with Adam." She headed off in the direction of Mr. Gray and my mother.

I turned to Cary. "Thank you for your assistance, but I'm afraid my mother and I must be going."

"I enjoyed meeting you, Ms. Singer. I'll

be around within the next day or so with that information you wanted."

I smiled. "Thank you." I caught Mom's eye just as Eleanor Ralston reached her and Mr. Gray. I gave a slight nod in the direction of the door. Mom said something to Mr. Gray and then made her way to the door.

We both wished we'd asked our cabbie to stay as soon as we stepped out into the cold. Being from San Francisco, we were used to taxis always being at the ready. That wasn't the case in this little section of the country.

Fortunately, there was a coffee shop across the street. We decided to call a cab from there so we could stay warm and drink hot cocoa while we awaited the cab's arrival.

Mom went to the counter to order our drinks, and I sat at a table near the window and dialed a local cab company. By the time Mom brought our drinks to the table, I was just finishing up the call.

I dropped my phone into my black clutch. "The dispatcher said he'll have someone here in about fifteen minutes," I said.

"All right. At least that should give us time to get started on our drinks."

"I don't want to take them with us," I said. "I shudder at the thought of hot cocoa all over that pretty gray suit."

She waved away my concern with a bejeweled hand. "That's what dry cleaners are for, love."

I took a sip of my cocoa. "Hot" was an understatement. It should've been called molten lava cocoa.

"I got a strange vibe at that place," I said, glancing over at the funeral home. "You know, stranger than just being at a funeral home, I mean."

"I do know what you mean. It was as if the only true mourner was Mr. Gray."

"I know. When I mentioned the sampler, all the granddaughter seemed to care about was its monetary value. When I told her there probably wasn't any, she told me to keep it."

Mom frowned. "It could still be worth a couple thousand. I wouldn't be surprised if she decides she wants it back to have it appraised, so don't frame it just yet."

"I won't. But isn't it a shame the family is interested only in divvying up the assets? Mrs. Ralston seemed like a really nice person."

"Nice people don't necessarily turn out nice children," Mom said. "And when money is involved, people do crazy things. I agree it's sad, though."

I saw our cab pull up outside. "Our ride is

here. What do you say we go home, get into our pajamas, make a big bowl of popcorn, and watch a movie?"

"An old movie?" Mom asked, standing and picking up her purse and her drink.

"We'll even watch a silent movie, if that's what you want."

We smiled at each other.

"Chaplin," we said in unison.

# CHAPTER SIX

Mom accompanied me to work the next morning. On her previous visits to Tallulah Falls, she had divided her time between the Seven-Year Stitch, my house, and other shops up and down the coast. But today she informed me that she intended to stay with me all day. I wasn't sure how long that would last without her going stir-crazy. Mom preferred sewing to embroidery, and I was afraid she'd get bored just keeping me company. I guess her guilt over my being caught with the type of medication used to kill Louisa Ralston had made her feel obligated to remain by my side.

For now, she was ensconced in one of the red club chairs playing tug-of-war with Angus. They were using his favorite blue-and-white braided rope toy, and it was hard to tell which of them was enjoying the game more. I had gotten some new metallic flosses in and decided to take this opportunity to set up a display for them on the counter.

I was ten minutes into my task when the bells above the door jingled, heralding the arrival of Carrington Ellis. He wore a navy pin-striped suit with a crisp white shirt, black wing-tip shoes, and a black fedora.

"Good morning, ladies," he said.

"Good morning," I said.

"Don't you look dapper?" Mom said. "You remind me of a young Cary Grant." She released the toy, and Angus took it and trotted over to lie by the window in the sun.

"Thank you so much. He's my namesake." He grinned and inclined his head. "But rather than naming me Archibald Leach Ellis — thank heavens — Mother named me Carrington Grant Ellis."

Mom laughed. "How delightful!"

"Thank you." He took a seat on the sofa facing away from the window, removed his hat, and placed it on the coffee table. "You speak as if you're a fan of Mr. Grant."

I quickly finished the floss display and joined Cary and Mom in the sitting area.

"I am a fan," Mom said. "Grant, Grace Kelly, Audrey Hepburn — I love all the icons of old Hollywood glamour."

"So do I," Cary said. "In fact, you looked as if you may have been channeling Grace

Kelly yourself last night. You looked very elegant. And, Marcy, I'd say you reminded me of Audrey Hepburn in a Givenchy LBD."

"Wow," Mom said, "I'm impressed with your fashion knowledge. How many men would know *LBD* for *little black dress,* much less that Givenchy was a popular designer for Audrey Hepburn?"

I was wondering if Cary might be gay.

Cary laughed. "Thank you. Wait a second — Beverly Singer. Are you *the* Beverly Singer? The *Queen of Claremont* costume designer?"

"I am."

"Oh, you're absolutely brilliant. You made Gloria Padget look wonderful as Queen Victoria."

Mom laughed. "No easy task, I assure you."

Cary and I laughed, too. Gloria Padget had been one of Mom's first "divas."

"How do you know so much about fashion and costuming?" Mom asked.

"It's what I do," Cary said. "I own a boutique. I once aspired to be a fashion designer myself, but I simply didn't have the talent. I can, however, recognize talent and appreciate beauty. I carry a lot of designers' clothing, both known and new."

"I'd love to check it out," I said. "Where's your shop?"

"It's only about thirty minutes away from here. It's called Carrington's." He reached into his breast pocket and handed me a business card. "I have something else for you, too." He took out an envelope. "Here is some information I was able to pull together on Millicent Connor, Aunt Louisa's great-grandmother, to go along with the sampler. As for Aunt Louisa herself, why don't I give the two of you a tour of her home so you can learn all about her yourselves?"

"I'd love that," I said. "And I know you would, Mom. Mrs. Ralston's house is beautiful."

"How's this?" Cary went on. "What if I take the two of you to dinner this evening and on to the house after we've finished dining?"

"That would be far too great an imposition," I said.

"It certainly would not," Cary said. "It would give me the opportunity to pick one of the greatest brains in Hollywood costume design today."

Mom beamed. "It's settled, then. What time should we be ready?"

■ ■ ■ ■

Vera Langhorne came into the shop minutes after Cary Ellis had driven away in his black Mercedes. She sniffed the air. "I smell men's cologne. It smells great . . . a Ralph Lauren scent, maybe?" She smiled at me. "Which of your admirers has been visiting, Marcy?"

"I believe this one favors Mom," I said, nodding toward my mother, still sitting in the red chair.

"Oh, hello, Beverly," Vera said. "I didn't see you here. Plus, I suppose, the scent of men's cologne addled my brain for a sec." She giggled. "I didn't know you'd be back so soon."

"Neither did I," Mom said, "but things just worked out this way."

"That's a lucky break for us, then," Vera said. "So who's *your* admirer?"

"His name is Carrington Ellis. He's a relative of the woman who collapsed in Marcy's shop earlier this week."

"Louisa Ralston," Vera said. "I didn't know her personally. It's such a shame that had to happen, though, for her family and for Marcy. He wasn't trying to make trouble, was he?"

"Not at all," I said. "In fact, the heirs are allowing me to keep the sampler Mrs. Ralston brought by, and I'm planning to frame it. I want to make a complete display using the sampler, a brief history of embroidery samplers, and a tribute to the women who created this particular sampler — Mrs. Ralston and her great-grandmother."

"What a wonderful idea. If there's anything I can do to help, please let me know." She moved over to the navy sofa facing the window. "I thought I'd stitch and visit for a while if that's all right."

"That's perfectly fine," I said. "I'll join you, and you can save Mom from being stuck talking only with me all day."

I took my current project — Riley's baby's christening gown — from behind the counter and sat on the sofa beside Vera. I'd brought it from home to try to finish up today.

Vera drew in her breath. "That's gorgeous!" She turned to Mom. "Isn't that beautiful?"

"It is," Mom said. "My daughter does terrific work."

"She certainly does." Vera took out her latest cross-stitch project — a pillowcase with a floral border across the hem. She was making herself a set.

"What are you working on?" Mom asked.

Vera proudly held up her pillowcase. "I'm saving my needlepoint project for class nights." She was halfway finished with this pillowcase, and it looked really pretty. Fortunately for Vera, the pattern was stamped onto the fabric and she didn't have to count her stitches. It really helped her out, especially since she loved to chat while she worked.

Mom made a fuss over Vera's needlecraft, and Vera blushed with pride. After all, it wasn't every day the favorite costume designer to A-list actress Clarissa LeBeau bragged on your work.

"You say you didn't know Mrs. Ralston," I said to Vera. "But do you happen to know her granddaughter, Eleanor?"

Vera paused in midstitch. "Eleanor Ralston . . . hmm . . . There was an Eleanor Ralston who used to work at John's bank as a teller. It was several years ago, while she was putting herself through college. Not much sticks out in my mind about her, except for the fact that I felt sorry for her. She seemed broke all the time. Either that, or she was stingy."

"What made you think that?" I asked.

"She never bought anything — no magazine subscriptions, no cookies, no whatever the kids were selling to support their causes." Vera resumed stitching. "One day I saw her leave in a brand-new car . . . a sports car. That's when I thought she might simply be stingy."

"That," Mom said, "or all her money went to pay for that sports car."

"You've got a point," Vera said. "I never had to worry much about money. Mom and Dad had plenty. I know that makes me very lucky. But I've seen how other young people have gotten themselves into bad situations by being unable to manage their money." She shrugged. "From what I've read in the paper, that won't be a concern for Eleanor Ralston any longer."

"No, I don't imagine it will." I resumed work on the gown, but my thoughts were on Eleanor Ralston. I wondered if she'd rebuffed her family's money to prove that she could stand on her own and now regretted it, or if she'd been denied the money because her family had thought she was irresponsible. Or, as Vera had said, the woman could've simply been a miser.

It was almost closing time, and Mom had taken Angus for a walk when Riley Kendall came in and threw herself onto one of the navy sofas with a dramatic sigh.

"Are you over that cold yet?" she asked.

"I'm feeling much better. Thanks."

"That's good."

"You seem down," I said. "What's wrong?"

"What's wrong?" She took off her shoes. "Look at how my ankles are swelling. My legs are starting to look like stovepipes."

"Nonsense. You look great. You've probably just been on your feet all day." I sat down on the opposite sofa, keeping the coffee table between us in case any of my common cold germs lingered. "Did you have court today?"

"Yes, and my current client is an idiot," Riley said. "Doesn't know when to keep his mouth shut and when to elaborate." She sighed again. "And Dad is depressed."

"Why?" I'd met Riley's father, Norman Patrick, a few months ago when I'd been investigating the death of Timothy Enright. He hadn't struck me as the type of person who'd be given to bouts of depression, despite the fact that he was only halfway into a three-year prison term.

"He's upset that he'll still be in prison when the baby is born," she said. "He says she won't even know him."

"It isn't like he's going to be incarcerated forever," I said. "He'll be out by the time the baby is walking, right?"

"Yeah, I guess. But not even Mom can cheer him up." She looked up at me. "Would you try? He likes you . . . says you remind him of Tinkerbell."

Visiting the prison wasn't high on my list of favorite things to do, but what could I say? "Well, my mom is visiting right now, and I hate to leave her."

"Couldn't you bring her along?" Riley asked. "Dad enjoys meeting new people."

*Oh, I'm sure Dad would enjoy meeting another woman. He's something of an old lecher.*

"Please?" Riley's eyes bored into mine.

How could I disappoint Riley? Besides, her dad might be able to give me more information on Adam Gray.

"Of course. I'll go up on Sunday. If Mom is still here, maybe she'll go up with me."

Riley smiled. "Thank you." She held up her feet again. "I'm already down to two-inch heels, but I'm afraid I'm going to have to take the plunge and start wearing flats."

Mom and Angus returned, and I asked Mom to put Angus in the bathroom. Riley liked Angus, but I was afraid that, given her condition, he might hurt her if he jumped up on her.

Mom dropped Angus off, then returned to the sitting area and joined Riley. "You look radiant."

Riley barked out a laugh. "You've got to be kidding. Or you're being kind."

"No, I mean it," Mom said. "You have a glow about you. I know it's hard and that this pregnancy is taking its toll on your body, but I can take one look at your face and see that deep down you have a serenity nothing can displace."

"She's good," Riley told me with a grin. "Thank you, Ms. Singer. I appreciate your kind words." She slipped her feet back into her shoes. "And thank you, Marcy. I'll tell Dad you'll be up on Sunday so he can be looking forward to it."

"Do you think he'd like to see some of the pieces I've done for the baby?" I asked.

"You know, I think he would," Riley said. "It might make him feel a little closer to her." She smiled. "You guys have a fun evening."

"You, too," Mom said. "Go home and let your husband pamper you for a while."

As soon as Riley left, Mom's smile faded and she looked at me sharply. "I thought her dad was in prison."

"He is."

"And you're planning to visit him on Sunday?"

"Yeah. Riley said he's really depressed

because he'll still be in prison when the baby is born. Maybe we can help cheer him up. And maybe he can tell us more about Adam Gray and give us more insight into Louisa Ralston and her relationships with her family members."

"We?" Mom asked.

"Sure . . . I mean . . . if you'll still be here Sunday and would like to go. It's a pretty good drive, and on the way home we can stop in Lincoln City for dinner. We'll make a day of it."

Mom closed her eyes and began rubbing her forehead. I went to let Angus out of the bathroom.

"So," I said when I returned, "would you like to go on Sunday?"

"No. But I'm not letting you traipse off to a prison on your own. I might never hear from you again."

# Chapter Seven

Cary took Mom and me to a lovely restaurant overlooking the ocean. The interior was paneled in light oak and tastefully decorated with marine images and photography. The floor was a burgundy carpet, and the tables had white cloths, white napkins with burgundy napkin rings, and fresh pink carnations. Small hurricane lamps on the tables bathed each of them in a warm glow.

We had already ordered and were awaiting our food when I happened to remember Mrs. Ralston's locket.

"Cary," I said, "I feel awful about this, but at the visitation for your aunt yesterday evening I forgot to tell Eleanor I found a locket in Mrs. Ralston's sewing kit."

He nodded. "I recall your mentioning a locket."

"I have it with me. Would you mind giving it to her?" I took it out of my purse and handed it to Cary.

"Not at all," he said as he took the locket. He opened it and held it up to the light. "This is a fantastic photo of Aunt Louisa. She looks so young and innocent. Yet there's something in her eyes, don't you think?"

Mom was sitting to Cary's left, so she leaned over to examine the picture. "There is something a little sad about her expression."

"The baby girl certainly looks happy, though," I said. "Look what a grin."

Cary frowned. "I wonder who this baby is. Aunt Louisa's only child was a boy . . . Eleanor's father."

"Maybe the child was ill," Mom said. "That could be why Louisa looks sad."

"You think the baby might've died?" I asked.

"Possibly." Mom took a drink of her water.

"But no one ever mentioned that Aunt Louisa had a child who'd died," Cary said. "I'll ask Mother about it." He closed the locket and placed it in his pocket as the waiter arrived with our meals.

Dinner was delicious. Both Cary and Mom had lobster tails, petit filets mignon, and baked potatoes. I had a salmon steak with perfectly crisp steamed vegetables. Mom had a glass of white wine with her meal, while Cary and I stuck with water, he because he was driving and I because I wanted to have all my faculties about me when we explored Louisa's fabulous house.

It was dark by the time we got to the Ralston home. It was stunning there in the moonlight, in all its Victorian splendor. But for some reason, the entire scene reminded me of those famous first lines from Alfred Noyes' "The Highwayman":

> The wind was a torrent of darkness
> among the gusty trees.
> The moon was a ghostly galleon tossed
> upon cloudy seas.

I had the fanciful notion that Louisa Ralston's ghost was standing behind the curtains in one of those dark upstairs windows. Louisa's ghost or her murderer. I noticed Cary staring at me intently, and I suppressed a shudder.

"Are you okay, Marcy?" he asked.

"I'm fine. It's a little chilly out here, that's all."

"Then let's get you ladies inside." He fished a key from his pants pocket and led the way up the steps to the door.

"Do you live here, Cary?" Mom asked.

"Nope. I keep a bachelor pad on the other side of town, but I dropped by Adam's office earlier today and borrowed his key. The reading of the will is to take place day after tomorrow, and then I suppose Eleanor will take possession of the home." He pushed open the door and flipped on the lights in the entryway before turning back toward us. "I imagine she'll sell it, and although it would be nice to have the Ralston family home, it's too much house for me."

Cary went on into the living room and turned on the lights. Mom and I followed.

"Look at this exquisite architecture," Mom breathed. "It's incredible."

I was looking at the Victorian furniture. A mahogany sofa with striped, floral upholstery sat near the fireplace. Two matching chairs were placed diagonally near each corner of the sofa so Mrs. Ralston's guests could sit around the fireplace and chat. A Persian rug lay on the polished mahogany floor between the sofa and the pair of chairs, and on the rug sat an oval marble-topped coffee table. Three matching end tables were located throughout the room. One by the window held a fern. There was also one by the sofa and another one by the chair to the sofa's right. These two tables held Victorian-style lamps featuring marble cherubs and frilly, ornate shades.

Cary gave us the grand tour of the house.

Mrs. Ralston had carried the Victorian theme throughout. The result was an elegant, classy home that looked as if it had stopped moving through time and was stuck somewhere before the turn of the century. It was gorgeous, but I felt it would be hard for me to make myself at ease in a house like this. I'd feel like I was living in a museum rather than a home.

"Has the home always been this well maintained?" Mom asked.

"No. If I'm not mistaken, it needed a lot of work when Aunt Louisa and Uncle Frank bought it."

"I understand it was an orphanage at one time," I said.

"Something like that, I believe," Cary said. "It changed hands several times before it became the dollhouse of Aunt Louisa and Uncle Frank. I think it took them two or three years to completely get it to the point it's at now."

"It was certainly worth the effort," Mom said.

We were passing through the dining room on our way back to the foyer when I noticed a piece of ribbon sticking out of a drawer on the hutch.

"Um . . . Cary," I said, "would it be all right if I tuck that ribbon back in the drawer? It's the only thing in the room that's out of place."

He chuckled. "Of course."

I opened the drawer and saw that the ribbon was stuck inside a photo album. "Do you think there are photos of little Cary in here?"

He smiled. "Take it out, and we'll see."

With a mischievous grin, I did as he instructed. The three of us gathered around the opulent dining room table to examine the old photos. There was indeed an adorable photo of little Carrington Ellis, smiling broadly with one front tooth missing.

"Even at that age you had a sense of fashion," Mom said. "See that impeccable suit and striped bow tie, Marcy?"

"I do," I said. "The kid had flair."

Cary laughed. "My mother likely had to bribe or threaten me to wear that suit for picture day."

We flipped through the book quickly, stopping only once or twice when Cary pointed out his parents and Louisa's husband. Near the end there was a photograph of the baby whose picture was in the locket with Louisa's. There was no indication of the baby's identity, but the date on the photograph was March 3, 1947. Cary took out the photo and flipped it over, but nothing was written on the back.

"Very curious," he murmured. "I really must talk with Mother and Adam to see if either of them knows anything about this child."

At home after Cary had dropped us off, Mom and I took another look at Mrs. Ralston's sampler.

"You need to get this framed as quickly as you can," Mom said. "Even if someone in the Ralston family does decide to ask you to return it, it's so old and fragile, I'm afraid it might fall apart if you don't."

"So am I."

"I'll be happy to drop it off at a frame shop tomorrow morning while you're working," she said, "if you'll point me in the right direction."

"Okay, I'll do that." I looked at the sampler a minute longer and then turned it over. "See why I'm so sure the original thread in the verse was torn out and replaced?"

She gently traced over the threads with her forefinger. "I do. The original thread was this rose color rather than the green." She frowned. "Wonder if Louisa — or whoever made the change — didn't like the verse that was there or if she simply redid the verse in this green thread for some reason? Or maybe this particular verse has meaning to the person who changed it."

"I feel there had to be a very pressing reason for someone to alter the original." I grabbed a pen and copied the verse onto a piece of paper before rewrapping the sampler in tissue paper. "Let's look this verse up on the computer and see what we find."

Mom shrugged. "Couldn't hurt."

We went upstairs to the guest bedroom that doubles as my home office. Angus trailed along behind us, unwilling to let Mom out of his sight for fear she might have a snack and neglect to give him most of it.

Mom sat down on the bed as I booted up the computer and typed the verse into a search engine. Angus lay on the floor beside the bed.

The verse was easy to find — even easier than I could have hoped. But my delight quickly turned to confusion tinged with a bit of creepiness. I turned to Mom.

"What, darling?" she asked upon noticing my expression.

"It's from *The Strange Case of Dr. Jekyll and Mr. Hyde.*"

"What is?"

"The verse," I said. "It's a quote from the

original novella by Robert Louis Stevenson."

"Why in the world would someone rip out the original verse in an antique sampler to replace it with a quote from a story about someone with a dual personality?" She propped the pillows against the headboard and lay back against them. Then she raised her eyes to the ceiling. "Read the quote to me again."

" 'His friends were those of his own blood or those whom he had known the longest; his affections, like ivy, were the growth of time, they implied no aptness in the object.' What do you think it means?"

"Since Mrs. Ralston came into the shop and asked you to help her find *ivy,* maybe Ivy is — as Ella Redmond suggested — a person Mrs. Ralston wanted you to help her find."

"But why me?" I asked. "I haven't been here even six months yet. I'm the last person in Tallulah Falls anyone should ask for advice . . . especially about people living here."

"You've got a point there. Still, Mrs. Ralston wasn't from here in town. Maybe she thought you were a native." She waved her hand as if she were shooing away a fly. "This entire situation is too strange, Marcella.

Why would the woman ask anyone other than a private detective for help if she was, in fact, trying to find a person? If she was merely looking for embroidery thread, then you and I are making much ado about nothing."

"And yet the fact remains that someone seems to have murdered her," I said.

"There is that." Mom sighed. "I'm sorry my little accident with Selena Roxanis got you pulled into this."

I went to sit beside her on the bed. "It didn't, Mom. The woman died in my shop. *That's* what got me pulled into this."

"Well, I didn't help matters by leaving that bottle of Selena's medicine in this nightstand."

I wasn't going to argue with her there. "I know I'm probably grasping at straws trying to determine what Mrs. Ralston wanted when she came into the Seven-Year Stitch the other morning. But I need to do *something* to try to figure this whole thing out. I need to find out who would want Mrs. Ralston dead. And I need to prove it wasn't me."

"I know. And I'm here to help you."

"I appreciate that, Mom, but will it interfere with the movie's production schedule?"

She shook her head. "It doesn't matter if

it does."

"It *does* matter. You haven't built up your reputation for the past thirty-two years to blow it now."

"I'm not blowing anything," she said. "My daughter is far more important than anything — than *everything.*" She smiled. "Besides, the movie is getting ready to wrap. My assistants can reach me by phone, e-mail, or videoconferencing, so I can still work without actually having to be on the set. Okay?"

"Okay."

"Tomorrow I'll have the sampler framed while you're working at the shop, and Sunday we'll go . . . to the prison." She arched a brow. "It'll be interesting to see what sort of friends you're making here in Tallulah Falls."

"I wouldn't exactly call Mr. Patrick a friend." I gave an awkward little laugh. "And actually, Mr. Patrick's location is a tad farther upstate from Tallulah Falls. But, still, you'll like him . . . probably. You've met Riley, and you like her, don't you? And I know you'd like his brother Maurice . . . or Moe — Captain Moe, that is. He owns a diner about a thirty-minute drive from here. He makes the best burgers. Maybe we can have dinner there before you leave town."

Mom closed her eyes. “When you babble, it worries me, Marcella. What aren’t you telling me?”

“Nothing,” I said, chewing on my bottom lip. “Not a thing.”

# Chapter Eight

Saturday was pleasant. There was no talk of murder or mayhem, Mom dropped the sampler off at a local frame shop, and business was brisk at the Seven-Year Stitch.

And now it was Sunday, and I was taking my mother to prison.

We'd left Angus in the backyard. The rain had turned to a mere drizzle, so I knew he'd be fine. He'd likely spend the day napping on the porch.

I did a side glance at Mom. She was completely nervous about this trip to the prison, but she was trying desperately not to let it show. "This isn't your first time visiting a prison, is it, Mom?"

"Oh, no . . . uh-uh. I've . . . I've visited them before. . . . You know, to research uniforms and inmates' clothing . . . that sort of thing."

I suddenly remembered where I got my babbling gene.

"Good . . . because we're here." I pulled up to the guard post outside the parking lot for the huge building. There was curled razor wire atop the building, and several lookout posts were stationed about.

Mom glanced around. "I thought you said this is a minimum-security facility."

"It is," I said. "But I suppose you can't be too careful. You never know when someone's going to go rogue, I guess."

I lowered the window as the guard leaned out of the shack and asked me to state my business. I gave him the name of the inmate that we were visiting. He looked at both our driver's licenses and took information about our car before pushing whatever button or buttons opened the gate to let us pass.

We got out of the Jeep, and I noticed Mom's eyes darting around like out-of-control Ping-Pong balls.

"Mom," I said, "it's okay. Really. I've done this several times."

"Several?"

"A few."

We walked through the first set of doors. Two guards wearing blue latex gloves went through our purses. Since we were wearing jeans, they also asked us to turn our front pockets inside out to ensure we weren't carrying anything in them. Our purses were then sent through the X-ray machine as we passed through the metal detector. We were given the okay to venture on ahead.

"See, Mom," I said, "it's not that much different from boarding an airplane."

"Right."

A female guard sitting behind a podium beyond the security checkpoint stood and unlocked the doors leading to the visitor information desk. She then closed the doors behind us, and I could hear the tumblers in the lock turning when she swiped her key through the automatic lock. Mom shot me a look that clearly said, *If there's a riot, we're locked in here with these people!*

The visitor information desk was basically a large steel countertop. Two more guards rechecked our driver's licenses, presumably to make sure we hadn't pulled a fast one on the guy in the guard shack. Then one of the guards instructed us to sign the logbook and to once again indicate the purpose of our visit. After we did that, the same guard opened a set of doors and led us down a hallway to the visiting area. The room was filled with vending machines and small round tables and chairs bolted to the floor.

Our guard nodded to one of the other guards stationed in the snack bar, and then he left us. There were no more than five people sitting in the area, so I spotted Mr. Patrick immediately. He gave me his sharky smile. I can't help it — there's just something about the man that reminds me of Bruce, the shark from *Finding Nemo.* Mr. Patrick is a large, beefy man with square-rimmed glasses and blue eyes that hold a sparkle of impishness.

"Hello, Tinkerbell," he said, standing to greet us. "Riley said you'd be visiting today. This enchanting creature must be your mother."

"Yep. Mr. Patrick, I'd like you to meet my mom, Beverly Singer."

"The pleasure is all mine," he said, taking one of Mom's hands and raising it to his lips. "Join me, won't you?"

We sat around the table.

"Heard about that business with Louise Ralston," he said. "I'm sorry you've suffered another blow so soon after Enright."

"Did you know Mrs. Ralston?" I asked.

"Sure did. Adam handled all the Ralstons' legal work, of course, but he talked to me a lot about Louisa."

"I got the impression they were more than business acquaintances," I said. "I think Mr. Gray genuinely cared about Mrs. Ralston."

"Cared about?" Mr. Patrick replied. "The guy was head over heels for her. He started working with the Ralstons right after he passed the bar exam and began practicing. Louisa Ralston was a real looker back then."

"Yes, she was," I said. "I saw her portrait hanging over the mantel."

"Even though she was married and had a good fifteen years on Adam, he was crazy about her." Mr. Patrick leaned back in his chair and steepled his fingers. "He's been married a couple times, but I don't think he ever quite got over being in love with Louisa."

"That's sad," Mom said.

"Indeed it is, Ms. Singer," Mr. Patrick said.

"Do you know anyone who had any grudges against the Ralstons?" I asked. "Louisa, in particular?"

He shook his head. "Sorry, Tink. I'm afraid I don't. I will play detective show with you, though, and ask you who had the most to gain from her death. Figure that out, and you've got a pretty good start."

"I guess the person with the most to gain financially would be the heir — Eleanor Ralston," I said.

"Has the will been read yet?" he asked.

"No."

"Then you don't know who the heir is." He smiled. "I've seen it time and again in my own practice. The so-called heirs never really know who will inherit until the will is read. Junior may already be spending Daddy's fortune only to discover that Daddy bequeathed everything to his alma mater."

"But other than financial gain," I said, "how else would anyone benefit from Louisa Ralston's death?"

"That's the answer you need to find."

"How about Cary?" Mom asked. "Do you know anything about him?"

Mr. Patrick's mouth turned down at the corners. "Cary is nice enough, I guess. Fancies himself something of a playboy."

"Really? I was thinking maybe he was gay," I said.

"Nah," Mr. Patrick said with a chuckle. "Just prissy and always putting on airs over clothes and manners and whatever."

"What about Eleanor?" I asked.

"Don't know anything about her," Mr. Patrick said. "What else have you got?"

"Only that Louisa or someone tore a verse out of an antique embroidery sampler and replaced it with a line from *The Strange Case of Dr. Jekyll and Mr. Hyde,*" I said. "Know why anyone would do that?"

He laughed. "I guess we all have our good and evil sides, Tinkerbell, but other than that, I don't have a clue."

"I have a surprise for you." I reached into my voluminous purse and pulled out the baby's christening gown. "I finished it just last night."

Mr. Patrick took the garment almost reverently. "This is for Riley's baby? My grandbaby?"

I nodded. "It's her christening gown."

His eyes welled with tears. "I won't be there to see her in it."

"Maybe not," I said, "but you know Riley will have someone videotape the ceremony from before it begins until well after it ends. And you'll be out of here in plenty of time to get to know your granddaughter. You'll likely even have the opportunity to do your share of diaper duty."

"I'll do it happily," he said with a smile. "Maybe wearing a gas mask, but I'll do it."

Mom and I stopped for dinner near Lincoln City on the way home. We decided to try an Italian restaurant, and fortunately we didn't need reservations. There was a slight wait, but we were seated within half an hour.

As we perused the menu, I caught Mom staring at a man sitting at the bar. I had to admit he wasn't bad-looking. He had sandy blond hair, neatly combed to the left . . . good build . . . nicely dressed in dark jeans, a striped shirt, and a brown blazer.

"He's a little young," I said, "but cougars *are* all the rage these days."

She huffed. "I'm not interested in the man, Marcella. Not *that* way. I think I saw him at the prison."

"You mean, you think he's one of the guards? Or was he visiting someone?"

"No, he wasn't actually *at* the prison. I saw him in the parking lot across the street. I noticed him because he was driving a really nice car — a Lexus — and he was standing outside his car, watching the prison. I thought maybe he was someone's lawyer and didn't want to park in the prison lot or something." She frowned. "And now he's here."

"What a coincidence," I said.

"I don't think so. Why would some guy come forty miles out of his way for a drink?"

"Maybe he's meeting someone, Mom."

"Or maybe he's following us."

The waitress arrived to ask if we'd decided on what we'd like to eat.

"Give us about five more minutes, please," Mom said.

"Sure." The waitress scurried off to another table.

"You don't seriously think we're being followed, do you?" I asked. "What possible reason would anyone have to follow us?"

"I don't know." She glanced at the man from over the top of her menu. "I just have a strange feeling about this."

"Well, let's decide on what we're having for dinner so we'll be prepared when the waitress returns, and we'll simply keep an eye on the man and see what he does."

"All right."

"He hasn't even looked over here," I said. "Are you sure he's the same guy you saw before?"

"Positive. I never forget a face. Names, yes; faces, never."

I wanted to point out that she could barely even see his face since he was in profile to us, but I didn't. Instead I said, "I think I'll have the fettuccini. How about you?"

"Chicken parmigiana," she said, closing her menu and looking at the man again.

"Okay," I said, exasperated that she wouldn't let this go. "Why would this man be following us, Mom? As I've already pointed out, he hasn't even looked over here."

Just as I got those words out of my mouth, he not only looked our way but raised his glass in a mock salute or greeting.

"If the waitress comes, give her my order," I said. I rose from the table and straightened my shirt.

"What are you doing?" Mom hissed. "You can't let him know we're on to him. Let's just go."

But she was too late. I was already headed his way.

"Hi," I said. "Do we know each other?"

"Not yet. I saw you looking at me and thought I'd let you know I'm interested, too," he said. He held out his hand. "Devon Reed."

I shook his hand. "Marcy Singer. I'm sorry if I gave you the wrong impression. It's just that my mom thought she'd seen you somewhere before."

"Oh, yeah? Where at?"

"At the prison about forty miles north of here."

He laughed.

"I'll tell her she was mistaken," I said.

He caught my arm as I turned to go back to the table. "She wasn't."

# Chapter Nine

I stared at him, not knowing what to say. Could Mom actually have been right? *Could* this guy have been following us?

"May I join the two of you?" he asked.

"Um . . . I guess so." I reasoned that we were in a public place and we would cause a major scene if he gave us any trouble.

Mom's eyes were nearly bulging out of her head when we reached the table.

"You were spot-on about the prison," I said, my voice not as level as I'd have liked it to be. "This is Devon Reed, and he says you did see him there."

I sat down in my chair, and Devon pulled a chair over from a vacant table.

"What were you doing there?" Mom asked.

"I'm a freelance journalist, Miss . . ."

"Singer," she said. "I'm Beverly Singer. So you were doing a story on the prison or something?"

"Something like that," Devon said. "Freelance journalism is an eclectic business. I was actually sent to the coast to do an article on entrepreneurs." He spread his hands. "The business magazine I'm writing the article for is interested in the various start-ups that have recently opened on the coast. I'm talking with shop owners to see what makes their businesses successful — that sort of thing."

"I'm an entrepreneur," I said.

"But why were you at the prison?" Mom asked, as if I hadn't spoken.

"I was hoping to do a piece on an industrial engineer who was arrested for insider trading last year," he said. "Thought it might be of interest to the same magazine." He grinned. "It's always best to pitch a new story while they're loving your old one."

"That's a valid point," Mom said. "Did you talk to the engineer?"

"Afraid not. He refused to see me." He shrugged. "It was worth a shot since I was driving through anyway. Where are you guys from?"

"We're from Tallulah Falls," I said. "And if you're doing a piece on entrepreneurs, I'd be happy to talk with you about my shop, the Seven-Year Stitch."

"The Seven-Year Stitch?" He chuckled.

"Cute name. I'm guessing it's a quilting store or something of that nature."

"Embroidery," I said quickly. "Plus, I have knitting and crocheting supplies, fabrics, pattern books, kits — anything the needlecraft connoisseur could possibly want. And I offer classes."

"The Seven-Year Stitch in Tallulah Falls," Devon said. "Thanks. I'll be looking you up. Any other entrepreneurs in the area I could talk with?"

"There's Sadie and Blake MacKenzie — they own MacKenzies' Mochas. And Todd Calloway owns the Brew Crew," I said. "I'm sure they'd all agree to talk with you."

"Sounds like easy money." He smiled. "Maybe I could simply do the article on the entrepreneurs of Tallulah Falls."

I fished a business card from my purse. "Here. This has the shop phone, my cell phone, and the shop address."

"Terrific, Marcy. Thank you. I'll call you when I get into town tomorrow," he said.

"Great. I'm looking forward to it."

The waitress arrived with our food. Devon stood and put the chair back at the empty table.

"If you'll excuse me," he said, "I'll let you ladies enjoy your meal." He nodded to the waitress, returned to the bar to pay his tab, and left.

After the waitress had our assurances that we had everything we needed, she, too, departed. As soon as she was gone, Mom started shaking her head.

"I don't like this," she said. "I still don't trust that guy. His story is just too . . . convenient."

"You've worked on too many movies, Mom." I squeezed her hand. "Relax. This could be some excellent free publicity for Sadie, Blake, Todd, and me."

In anticipation of Devon Reed's coming by to interview me, I wore a red pantsuit with a beige silk blouse and taupe platform pumps to work on Monday. Mom wore jeans, a chunky ivory sweater, and a sour expression. She still wasn't convinced that Devon was on the level. In fact, she was convinced that he *wasn't.*

Even Angus could tell Mom's mood was off that morning. Rather than try to engage her in playing with him, he took his toy and retreated to his bed behind the counter.

I'd called both Sadie and Todd after Mom and I got home yesterday evening and told them about the article. Like me, Sadie was thrilled. Todd took more of a *that's great if it works out* attitude.

We'd been at the shop less than thirty minutes when Ted Nash arrived. He'd met Mom when she visited before.

"Good morning, Ted," I said. "You remember my mom."

"Of course. How are you, Ms. Singer?"

"I'll be better when this whole Louisa Ralston thing is cleared up," she said. "Have you heard anything? Was my testimony sufficient to dispel the police officers' suspicions about Marcy?"

"That's actually why I'm here," Ted said. "As you know, we're not handling the investigation, but our department works fairly closely with Tallulah County. That, and Manu has been keeping an eagle eye on this case." He sat down on one of the sofas, while Mom and I chose the chairs. "The investigators you spoke with, Ms. Singer, followed up with Selena Roxanis. She confirmed your story about her spilling her purse in the wardrobe room."

"They thought I was lying about that?" Mom asked. "They thought I *stole* the pills from her?"

"They have to confirm everyone's stories, ma'am. It was nothing against you personally."

Mom settled back in her chair, somewhat appeased. "But is Marcy still a suspect?"

"I'm afraid they still haven't ruled anything out," Ted said. "They're unable to find anyone else with a connection to Louisa Ralston who takes Halumet or has access to the drug."

"But what about the streets?" Mom asked him. "Can't people buy just about any drug they want off the streets . . . or over the Internet?"

"Yes, ma'am, they can. But until they find someone with sufficient motive, they can't get a search warrant for computers or anything of that nature." Ted leaned forward and looked at Mom earnestly. "But they're looking, Ms. Singer. And, unofficially, so are we."

"Thank you, Ted," I said.

He gave me a reassuring smile. "We'll figure this out, Marcy."

"I know." *I hope.*

"You both look great, by the way," Ted said. "Big plans after work?"

"Hopefully, big plans *at* work," I said.

Mom scoffed. "Yesterday I was certain we were being followed, so Marcy went over and confronted the guy. He gave her some song and dance about being a freelance journalist doing an article about entrepreneurs on the Oregon coast."

"I gave him my business card, told him

about Todd and the MacKenzies, and he said he might come by today to interview me," I told Ted. "He said he might interview all us local entrepreneurs for his article. I think it would be super publicity for us and for Tallulah Falls in general."

"I think Marcy is being naive," Mom said. "I believe the guy made up the story to cover his tracks. He was following us — I'm sure of it."

Ted took out his notepad and pen. "Give me his name. I'll check him out."

"I was going to Google him last night, but I didn't have time," I said. "I'm sure there's no need for a background check. Besides, there are better ways you could spend your time."

Ted grinned. "That's true enough."

He glanced at Mom and back and then back at me. I know he'd have said something flirtatious had she not been sitting there. Just the thought of my unintentional double entendre made me blush and made him laugh.

"He said his name was Devon Reed," Mom said, "and he was driving a silver Lexus LFA."

Ted gave a low whistle. "Maybe I should get into freelancing."

"Or the con man game," Mom said.

"What makes you think this man was following you?" Ted asked.

"We saw him at the prison, and then —"

"The prison?" Ted interrupted. He hated it when I went to the prison.

"Yes," I said. "Riley asked me to go up to the prison and visit her dad. She said he's been really down lately. I showed him the christening gown I embroidered for Riley's baby, and it made him cry."

"Anyway, the prison is where I first saw this so-called Devon Reed," Mom said. "He was parked across the street and was standing outside his car when we arrived."

"So he was at the prison when you got there," Ted repeated.

"Exactly," I said. "Which means he couldn't possibly have followed us to the prison." I shot Mom a triumphant glance, but she merely rolled her eyes.

"But when we stopped for dinner forty miles away, he was there, too," Mom said.

"I think it's just a stroke of serendipity," I said.

"Maybe," Ted said. "But I will check up on this guy to see if he's legitimate."

"Thank you," Mom said.

After Ted left, I sat at the counter and got to work on Riley's burp cloth. It was cute.

It had pink, blue, and yellow blocks around all four borders, and upon completion there would be fringe around the edges. I would have liked to work on the *Boulevard of Broken Dreams* piece, but I couldn't do that while Mom was visiting, since it was to be her birthday gift.

Mom took Angus for a walk. While they were gone, Ella Redmond came into the shop. She looked more cheerful than she had on the other occasions that I'd seen her. Rather than black or drab gray clothing, she was wearing jeans and a light blue sweater that played up her blue eyes.

"Hey, Ella. What brings you by this morning?"

"I'm looking for some ribbon," she said. "I'd like either a pretty floral or maybe a single-color pastel."

I put my work down and led her to where the spools of ribbon were displayed. "What type of project is this for?"

"My mother gave me an eyelet table runner that has a ribbon trim around it. The ribbon has become really frayed, and I want to replace it."

I picked out some thin ribbons I thought could be easily worked through the eyelet. "In pastels, I have this lovely pink, a seafoam, a lemon, and a peach that would be thin enough to thread through eyelet. And here are some florals. I particularly like this one with the violets."

"Oh, I like the violets, too," Ella said. "I think I'll take that one."

We went back to the counter. As I rang up her purchase, Ella looked at the burp cloth.

"This is sweet," she said.

I laughed. "I've done so many sweet projects for Riley's baby, I'm afraid they're going to give me cavities. After this, I think I'll look for something a little edgier."

Ella laughed, too. "You look very nice today, by the way. Not that you don't look nice every day, but I notice you're more dressed up today than usual. Anything special going on?"

I told Ella about the man Mom was convinced was following us but who turned out to be a freelance journalist seeking Oregon coast entrepreneurs to interview. "What luck, right?" I asked.

"Absolutely," she said. "I think that's terrific. Have you heard from the guy yet?"

"Not yet."

"You will." She smiled. "You deserve to have some good things come your way."

Just before Ella left, Mom and Angus returned from their walk. I introduced the two women, but Mom reminded me she'd met Ella at the needlepoint class the night of Mrs. Ralston's visitation.

"That's right," I said. "I'm sorry, Ella."

"No need to apologize," she said. "I know you've had a lot on your mind lately. Your interview with this journalist will be a good break for you . . . give you something to think about other than Mrs. Ralston and that horrible situation."

"Yeah. Thanks."

Ella said her good-byes and left the shop.

"So you heard from Mr. Reed?" Mom asked.

"Not yet," I said. "I was just telling Ella about the possibility of being interviewed for a magazine article."

Mom sighed. "Darling, I can get you all kinds of publicity. I know a lot of people —"

"You know a lot of people in the *entertainment* business, Mom. Besides, I want to do this on my own. Don't you think there's *anything* I can do on my own? Without someone being there to hold my hand?"

"I find you very capable. I'm just offering my help. Is that such a bad thing?"

I was saved from answering by the phone ringing. It was Devon Reed. He wanted to know what time he could come by and interview me.

# Chapter Ten

Mom's lips tightened as soon as she saw Devon Reed's silver Lexus pull up outside. Today he was wearing jeans, a white polo, and a brown leather bomber jacket. As he approached the shop door, he took off his sunglasses and put them in his pocket. Considering there was precious little sunshine outside, I thought that was a good idea. Still, I supposed the man wanted to look cool — and he did.

I was sitting with Mom on the navy sofa poring over the script for her next project. I started to jump up and try to appear busy, but I figured what was the use? I was too excited about the interview to do anything but rehearse answers to imagined questions floating around in my head, anyway.

"Hello, Marcy . . . Ms. Singer. How are you both today?" Devon asked, standing just inside the shop and surveying his surroundings. He nodded toward Jill. "What's with the mannequin?"

I cleared my throat. "She's . . . um . . . more of a prop than anything. Since I named the store the Seven-Year Stitch, I thought it would be cool to have a Marilyn Monroe look-alike in the shop. You know, because of the movie *The Seven-Year Itch*?"

"Never saw it." He strolled around, taking in all the displays and nodding occasionally. I couldn't tell from his expression whether the nods were appreciative or critical. I glanced at Mom. Her expression was windowpane clear. She was flat-out disgusted.

"Feel free to take whatever photographs you'd like," I said.

"Yeah," Devon said, "I'll do that before I leave." He smiled and took a recorder from his pocket. "Shall we get down to business?"

I nodded. "Sure."

"Let's sit over here on this couch across from your mother," he said. "That way, Ms. Singer, if you have anything to add, you can jump right in."

"Thanks," Mom said drily. I noticed she'd closed the script and turned it facedown beside her on the sofa. She was ever vigilant in maintaining the confidentiality of her clients' projects.

Devon turned on the recorder. "This is Devon Reed talking with Marcy Singer, proprietor of the Seven-Year Stitch, an embroidery specialty shop. Also with us is Marcy's mother, Beverly Singer. Marcy, how long have you been in business here in Tallulah Falls?"

"Only a few months," I said, "but business has been booming. Tallulah Falls is a generous, welcoming community, and the people here have been very supportive of me and the Seven-Year Stitch."

"This, despite the fact that there seems to be some sort of curse hanging over your store?" he asked.

"I . . . um . . . Excuse me?" I replied.

"Well, first you found a man dead in your storeroom shortly after you opened — during your first week, in fact, wasn't it? And now there has been another death in your store. Isn't that correct?"

Slack-jawed, I turned to look at Mom, but she was already coming to my defense.

She stood up and snatched the recorder from Devon's hand. Glaring at him, she snapped the recorder off. "What's the meaning of this? My daughter thought you were coming here to interview her about her shop and her experiences as an entrepreneur."

"But I am, Ms. Singer," Devon said. "I believe my readers would be interested in knowing how Marcy has weathered these unusual storms."

"She's weathered them with strength and dignity," Mom said. "And she doesn't need someone like you to come along and undermine everything she's worked so hard to build."

"Mom, it's okay," I said.

"No," Devon said. "Your mother is quite right. I overstepped here, and I apologize. I'll take that out of the interview."

"I'd prefer not to continue the interview just now," I said. I'd been blindsided by Devon's initial line of questioning, and now I didn't feel I could trust him, either.

"I understand." He rose and held his hand out for the recorder. Mom slapped it into his hand hard enough to hurt, but Devon didn't flinch. "I'll talk with the other entrepreneurs you told me about and stop back by before leaving town."

"I knew there was something untrustworthy about that man," Mom muttered under her breath as Devon walked out the door.

Rather than get into his car, he consulted a card he'd taken from his pocket and strode down the street toward MacKenzies' Mochas.

"Should I call and warn Sadie?" I asked. "She's as excited about being interviewed as I was."

Mom shook her head. "There's no time. Besides, it'll be interesting to see if he questions Sadie and Blake about the chamomile tea that Mrs. Ralston tasted just prior to her collapse."

"Yeah . . . I guess. It's terrible, though, that I got everyone's hopes up about this guy, his article, and our free publicity, and he winds up being a total jerk." I fought to hold back tears.

"I'm sorry," Mom said.

"I should've listened to you," I said. "You smelled a rat all along."

She shrugged. "When you get to be my age, you get cynical. I'm glad you're still too young to be suspicious of everyone."

"Too young or too naive?" I sighed. "I wonder what — if anything — Ted will turn up on Devon Reed."

Mom didn't have the opportunity to comment on that. A customer came in wanting a fantasy or mythological cross-stitch kit. By the time I'd helped the young lady find a design featuring a unicorn and a medieval princess standing in a moonlit meadow, Mom had gone back to studying her script and penning notes in the margin.

After the customer left, I resumed work on Riley's burp cloth and kept glancing surreptitiously out the window to see what Devon might be up to. I didn't catch sight of him, but his car was still parked outside the shop.

Had I been too hasty in ending the interview? Maybe he *did* think his readers would be interested in how a new entrepreneur would handle two such potentially devastating blows in the short amount of time she'd been in business. Maybe he'd intended to slant the article to make me look like a real trouper . . . someone who had a dream and was determined to make that dream come true no matter what.

Or maybe he'd meant to make me look guilty. He had to know that reporting the occurrence of two murders in my shop within a few months of each other would be detrimental to my business. Even I knew — and I wasn't a journalism major — that when you're trying to portray local entrepreneurs in a favorable light, you accentuate the positive. Unless he was intent on portraying us in an *unfavorable* light.

Todd came into the shop following his interview with Devon. "How'd your interview go?" he asked me.

"It didn't go very far," I said. "He started asking questions about my finding a corpse in the storeroom my opening week and then about Mrs. Ralston's death."

Todd frowned. "Are you serious?"

Mom looked up from her script. "He's lucky I didn't shove that recorder up his nose."

"How did your interview with him go?" I asked.

"Fine," Todd said. "He didn't ask me anything out of the ordinary. Just a few basics like, 'How long have you been in business?' 'How do you keep customers coming back?' Things like that."

"He didn't ask you anything about Marcy?" Mom asked.

"Come to think of it, he did ask how long I've known her," Todd said. "But that was about the extent of it." He winked at me. "I told him I hadn't known Marcy nearly long enough."

"Where did he go after talking with you?" I asked.

"I think he was going to speak with the aromatherapy woman, Nellie Davis," Todd said. "I doubt he'll get much out of her, though."

"Oh, I don't know about that," I said. "After Todd Enright died, she raked me over the coals. She'll probably have plenty to tell

Mr. Reed if he asks any questions about me."

"I'll talk with Alfred — he's my attorney and lifelong friend —" Mom explained to Todd, "and see if we can get some sort of injunction against this guy if we have to. I rather doubt it, but it won't hurt to ask."

Todd sat beside Mom on the sofa. "Do you think these interviews are merely a ruse to get to Marcy in some way?"

"I don't know," Mom said. "I've racked my brain trying to figure out what's up with that man."

"Speak of the devil," I said softly. Devon Reed was entering the shop.

"Hi, guys," Devon said, his smile encompassing all of us. "Marcy, I'd really like to finish up that interview. I have some great stuff from Mr. Calloway there and from your friends Blake and Sadie."

"How about Nellie?" I asked. "Did she have anything to say?" I figured she'd told Devon plenty about the bohemian who she thought ran Tim Enright out of business with an artsy shop that would draw more customers than Mr. Enright's hardware store.

"Oh, sure," Devon asked. "I found her to be particularly loquacious and accommodating."

"I'll bet. Did you take her a little something from the Brew Crew?" I asked.

Devon laughed. "Nope. I didn't get her drunk. She did ask me to dinner, so maybe she just liked me."

"Maybe," I said.

"I told her I have plans for dinner. I hope you won't make me out to be a liar," he said.

I frowned, not following him.

"I told her I was taking you to dinner to finish up our interview," Devon said.

"I'm afraid I can't," I said. "Mom is only here for a few more days. I couldn't possibly —"

"Nonsense," Mom interrupted. "Todd and I will join you . . . that is, if you don't have any other plans, Todd."

"What? But —"

"I don't, and if I did I'd change them," Todd said, interrupting me. "I think this evening will be a lot of fun."

Devon looked as if he was about to argue that point but then changed his mind. "Yeah . . . it'll be . . . fun. Should I pick all of you up at Marcy's house, then?"

"Why don't we have dinner at MacKenzies' Mochas," Mom said, "and all of us simply meet there?"

I continued staring at Mom as if she'd just sprouted a second head.

"That way," she continued, "you'll have Blake and Sadie on hand if you think of any other questions for them." She looked at me. "What do you think?"

"I . . . I guess."

"Devon, what do you think?" Mom asked.

"Fine," he said tightly. "I'll meet all of you at MacKenzies' Mochas at . . . say, six o'clock?"

"It's a date," Mom said with a smile.

"See you then." Devon plodded out to his car, got in, slammed the door, and sped off.

Mom looked at Todd and me with a barely concealed grin on her face. "Humph, I'd almost think he hadn't wanted to include us in his invitation, Todd."

"I, too, got that impression, Ms. Singer." Todd feigned a pompous voice. "But, of course, we must be mistaken. How could he not desire our company?"

"Quite right, my dear. Quite right."

"Mom, what's up with you?" I asked. "I thought we were through with that guy."

"Not yet," Mom said. "We still don't know what he's up to . . . and I intend to find out."

# Chapter Eleven

I took Angus home, fed and walked him, touched up my makeup, and then returned to the shop. From there, Mom and I went over to MacKenzies' Mochas. I love stepping into MacKenzies'. The smell is intoxicating: coffee, cinnamon, vanilla, hazelnut, chocolate — all those scents blend into ambrosia for the nose.

Todd was already there and was standing at the counter talking with Blake. He was still wearing jeans but had changed into a blue-and-white-striped dress shirt. Blake, looking boyishly mischievous with a lock of blond hair falling into his eyes, raised a brow at Mom and me when we walked in. He knew something was going on, but I couldn't tell if he knew quite what it was. If he did, I wished he would explain it to me.

"Hi, there," Sadie said, coming from our left with an empty serving tray in her hand. She wore black jeans and a black-and-white tuxedo-style blouse. "What a nice surprise. I didn't know you guys were coming in this evening."

"Actually, neither did we until just a little while ago," I said. "Todd's joining us."

Sadie shot me a look full of questions she knew I couldn't answer at the moment.

"So am I."

I turned to see that Devon Reed had just walked in. If Sadie's dark brown eyes were full of questions before, they were practically swimming in them now.

"Okay . . . um . . . table for four, then," she said, setting the tray on the counter. "Follow me."

Todd fell into step beside us, and we trailed along behind Sadie like a group of schoolchildren following their teacher. She led us to a table that was within easy viewing distance of the counter.

She took our drink orders, said she'd bring the menus with our drinks, and hurried back up to the counter.

"Is the food good here?" Devon asked. "I'm famished."

"It's excellent," I said.

"Interesting decor they have," Devon said, glancing around the room.

"Yep," said Todd. "It was a bar before

Blake and Sadie converted it into a coffee shop."

The long, polished bar remained and now served as the counter. Oak tables and chairs were placed throughout the rest of the shop. On shelves behind the bar, there were MacKenzies' Mochas mugs, house-blend coffees for sale, chocolate-covered coffee and espresso beans, biscotti, and other packaged goods. Covered cake plates situated along the bar displayed the day's muffins, pies, and other pastries. The counter behind the bar was where the coffeemakers, cappuccino machines, and espresso machines were located. The kitchen was in the back.

Devon nodded. "The MacKenzies mentioned that during their interview. Which reminds me, I need to finish yours, Marcy . . . but not until after dinner, of course."

I gave him a small smile. "Of course. What photographs did you take here for your article?"

"I photographed the charming couple behind the counter. I thought it would be good to show readers our entrepreneurs hard at work, along with some of the products they're selling on the shelves behind them," Devon said.

"That's clever," I said. "Any others?"

"No," Devon said. "I think that photograph will be sufficient to convey the friendly ambience of the shop."

"How about Todd and the Brew Crew?" Mom asked. "I hope you got some interesting photos there."

"I believe I did," Devon said. "Wouldn't you agree, Todd?"

Todd shrugged. "Yeah, I think they'll be okay."

"Once again, Marcy, you're our holdout." Devon smiled at me. "But we're planning on remedying that as soon as possible."

Sadie brought the drinks and menus. After handing them out, she turned to me. "I could use your opinion on something." She looked around at Mom, Todd, and Devon. "Do you guys mind if I steal Marcy away for a minute? I promise I'll have her back in just a sec."

Everyone nodded noncommittally, and Sadie spirited me away to the kitchen.

"What do you need my opinion on?" I asked, knowing full well she didn't need my opinion on anything.

"Has the entire world gone nuts? That's what I need your opinion on."

I tilted my head. "Possibly."

"So what's really up?" she asked.

I explained how my interview went and Mom's reaction. "And then Mom totally blew me away by accepting *my* dinner invitation from Devon and inviting Todd to come along, too."

Sadie giggled. "Your mom is wild. What is she up to?"

"With Mom, you can never tell. She says she's trying to see what Devon Reed is up to, but I'd just as soon we'd told him to forget about the interview as well as dinner and simply be done with the whole mess."

"No, I'm with your mom. I think she's right."

I clamped my lips together. "Please tell me he didn't give you guys the third degree in your interview."

Sadie flipped her palms. "I don't know that I'd go as far as to say he gave us the third degree, but he did ask several questions about you."

"Such as?"

"How long we've known you, what we think about the string of bad luck you've been having —"

"But I haven't been having bad luck as far as business goes," I interrupted. "And that's what he's *supposed* to be interested in."

"That's why I think your mom is right. We need to discover his true motives." She started to step out of the kitchen but turned back. "You don't think he's a tabloid reporter, do you?"

"No," I said. "Why would a tabloid reporter care about me?"

"Maybe it's your mom he's after." Sadie shrugged. "I mean, what if the chick who dumped her purse in the wardrobe room and lost her pills is paying this guy to get something on your mom? You know she and your mom have to be like two circling wolves."

"I never thought of that angle — and never would have if you hadn't brought it up — but I suppose it could be possible."

"Think about it," Sadie continued. "If Devon had something to hold over your mom's head — like running a story that could jeopardize your business — then he could blackmail her into laying off Selena Roxanis." She inclined her head. "Or if he isn't working with her, he could use this to try to get your mom to give him information about the actors she's working with. Tabloid reporting pays awfully well."

"Still, that's pretty far out there, Sadie. I mean, everybody in Tallulah Falls knows I found Timothy Enright in the storeroom, but they still come in and shop. How could Devon threaten to use a story against me that everyone in town already knows? Where's the logic in that?"

"He could put a bad spin on things . . . maybe make people think you had something to do with people dropping dead in your store . . ." She let the implication hang there.

I took a deep breath. "Yeah, I don't know. As I've already said, I just want to put this entire mess behind me. So the sooner we get this dinner over with, the better."

Sadie and I returned to the table. I sat down and Sadie took our food orders. Lucky for me, I always order the chicken salad on a croissant, so I didn't have to take up more time ordering. I didn't want to be responsible for holding everyone else up.

"So, Ms. Singer," Devon said, "what do you do for a living?"

"I'm a seamstress," Mom said.

I'd just taken a sip of my diet soda, and at that statement I strangled on it. My eyes watered, and I sat there coughing while Mom patted me on the back.

"Try to breathe, darling," she said. "Maybe you should take another drink."

"I think you should have a drink of water," Devon said, hopping up from his seat. He then took me by the arm and steered me up to the counter. "Blake, may we please have a glass of water?"

"You okay, Marce?" Blake asked as he opened a bottle of water and poured it into a glass.

I nodded. "I got strangled, that's all." I gratefully accepted the water and took a drink. "That does help, Devon. Thank you."

"No problem," he said. "But now that I have you away from your mom and Todd, what gives? I understand why you cut the interview short and didn't want to continue, but now I feel I'm getting the runaround. Care to explain?"

Blake took a damp cloth and began wiping down the counter near us. Since he hadn't been privy to the conversation in the kitchen, I imagined he, too, was wondering what was going on.

"Mom doesn't trust you, Devon . . . and, frankly, after you began asking me all those questions about the body in the storeroom and the incident with Louisa Ralston, I'm not sure I trust you, either."

"I explained that to you," he said. "I wanted to illustrate how you've persevered despite those unusual circumstances."

"But it made me feel as if you were sabotaging me."

"I'm sorry." Devon placed his hands on my shoulders. "Can we start again? I won't mention either the first incident or Louisa Ralston in my interview. I promise."

I smiled slightly. "Okay."

Devon dropped his hands. "As a matter of personal curiosity, though, I would like to know what Mrs. Ralston was doing out that morning when she was obviously unwell. Wouldn't you?"

I finished off my glass of water. I could tell Todd was considering coming to see if I was all right. "We need to get back. Our food should be out any minute."

"Right. But you have my card, don't you? If you'd like my help figuring out what the deal was with Mrs. Ralston, let me know. I'm planning on doing some investigating on my own, anyway." He held up his hand. "And it won't have anything to do with your interview or your shop. I simply want to know — as an investigative journalist — what compelled Mrs. Ralston to leave her home to visit Tallulah Falls during heavy rains when she was on the verge of collapse." He turned and started back toward the table.

"Wait," I said. "I would like to know."

"Then allow me to drive you home after dinner. We can chat . . . just the two of us."

"I can't. Mom can't drive the Jeep. She says it's too big. Plus she hates to drive, period."

"How about tomorrow, then?" Devon asked.

"That could work. She was with me at the shop all day today, so I imagine she'll want to stay at home for a while tomorrow . . . especially since we have class tomorrow night."

"Good. I'll call before I come by."

We returned to the table and sat down. Todd and Mom began talking at once.

"Feeling better?" Todd asked.

"What took you so long?" Mom asked.

"Everything is fine," I said. "Devon and I have decided that since he'll be in town for a few more days, we'll simply enjoy dinner tonight and he can finish the interview later in the week. Right, Devon?"

"Absolutely. I let work consume too much of my time, anyway. It'll be nice to have a dinner conversation without mentally taking notes for a change."

"What's the deadline for your article?" Mom asked.

"I've got plenty of time," Devon said. "The editor is really flexible. Tell me about your job, Ms. Singer. Is being a seamstress pretty seasonal — proms and weddings — or is it year-round work?"

"I manage to stay busy pretty much all

the time," Mom said.

Fortunately, Sadie brought our food, saving Mom from having to further elaborate on her career as a humble seamstress.

When we first got into the Jeep to drive home, we initially shivered and refrained from talking. The temperature had dropped considerably while we'd been having dinner. But as soon as the heater kicked in, so did Mom's mouth.

"What did Devon say to you when he had you over there at the counter all to himself?" she asked.

"He basically asked me why I seemed reluctant to give him the interview, and I told him we didn't trust him after he began asking all those questions about Timothy Enright and Louisa Ralston."

"How did he react to that?"

I shrugged. "He tried again to convince me that he wasn't out to cast the Seven-Year Stitch in a bad light, and he requested another opportunity for the interview. He promised that this time there would be no mention of the *unfortunate events* and that he'd keep them out of the article."

"Do you believe him?"

"I'm not sure, Mom. He seems sincere,

and you saw how cordial he was over dinner."

"Yes, darling, but everyone can be cordial to get what they want."

"Which is what?"

She sighed. "I still haven't figured that one out. Do you intend to grant him a second interview?"

I did, but I didn't want Mom to know that. To buy time, I said, "Let's wait and see what Ted has to say. If he found proof that Devon Reed is who he claims to be, then I see no reason not to grant him the interview. If he isn't who he claims to be, I'll need to decide whether or not to confront him with that information."

# Chapter Twelve

I arrived at the Seven-Year Stitch the next morning about half an hour before the store was scheduled to open. I'd left Mom and Angus in bed. Last night before turning in, Mom had instructed me not to get her up this morning. She said she would wake up, dress, and bring Angus to the shop at her leisure. And she'd said she planned to go by the frame shop to see if the sampler was ready to be picked up.

I flipped on the lights, yawned, and greeted Jill. It was a peaceful morning. The rain had slackened, and I'd even spotted a rainbow on the way to work. The birds were trilling; the waves were crashing. . . . The day had all appearances of being a good one, but I had a nagging feeling telling me not to get my hopes up.

I took out my cell phone, deposited my purse and tote bag on the shelf behind the counter, perched on the maple stool, and called Ted Nash.

"Nash," he said.

"Morning, Ted. It's Marcy."

"Hi, there." Now he had a smile in his voice. "Everything all right?"

"Yep, everything's fine. I was just wondering if you were able to find out anything about Devon Reed."

"I'm afraid not," he said. "A simple Internet search turned up several Devon Reeds, but it's almost impossible to follow up on credentials based on a name, occupation, and description."

"So you didn't find any articles by a Devon Reed?" I asked. "My Google search didn't turn up any, either."

"No. If we had his Social Security number or fingerprints to run through AFIS, the FBI's fingerprint system, it would be a lot easier."

"Yeah, I know. But even if you did, he may not be in the system," I said.

"Spill it. Did he do something to freak you out, or what?"

I sighed. "A little." I explained about the interview and his immediately touching on the incidents with Timothy Enright and Louisa Ralston. "What do those isolated incidents have to do with my running a shop?"

"I don't know. I do advise you to err on the side of caution. Always."

"Thanks."

"Let me know if you need anything else," he said.

I assured him I would, and we ended the conversation. I went into my office and put some water into my single-cup coffeemaker. While the coffee was brewing, I went into the storeroom to get some supplies that needed to be restocked out on the floor: embroidery hoops, needles, yarns. White yarn, in particular, had been a big seller this weekend, both with the knitters and with the customers who crochet. I hadn't asked what was up with all the white yarn. Knowing Riley, I could imagine that she'd commissioned them all to make things for Baby Kendall.

I arranged the items on the floor and straightened up bins that had become untidy on Saturday. I had just poured my freshly brewed coffee when, a little surprisingly, Eleanor Ralston came in.

"Good morning, Eleanor," I said. "Would you like some coffee?"

"No, thank you." She gazed around the shop. "I hope you don't mind my coming. I wanted to see where Grandma spent her last morning."

"Oh, I don't mind at all." I set my coffee on the counter and came around to Eleanor's side. "Would you care to sit down?"

"I would, actually. Thank you." She sat on the navy sofa facing the window. "You have a beautiful shop."

"Thanks." I could tell she'd been crying. Maybe she'd still been in shock or something over her grandmother's death at the funeral and was only now experiencing grief at her loss. "Is there anything you need? Anything I can get you?"

"No," she said. "Just . . . would you sit down and tell me about Grandma that morning? Did she seem happy?" Eleanor was wearing a gray trench coat and a white scarf and hat. She kept twisting the scarf around her fingers.

"She did seem happy," I said, sitting down beside her. "I think she wanted to do something with the sampler. Maybe she wanted me to make her a pattern from it so she could reproduce it or something. We didn't get a chance to discuss it."

"No, I don't suppose you did." She shook her head. "I know I should've talked with you before now, but things have been so crazy and there was so much to do. I wasn't myself at all on the evening of the funeral."

"I understand completely."

"I feel as if I've been numb for days," she said. "Just sort of moving on autopilot, you know?"

"I do know. Losing my grandmother a few years back was devastating."

"D-did she say anything?" Eleanor asked. "I know you're aware that the police think someone poisoned Grandma or that she accidentally ingested some drug that made her have a heart attack. I'm just wondering if she said anything before she collapsed . . . if there was any indication that anything was wrong."

"Not at all. She asked me to help her find ivy," I said, with a slight lift of my shoulders. "Does that mean anything to you?"

"Not to me. If she was working on an embroidery project, I suppose that might've been the color of some thread she needed."

"I thought about that, too," I said.

"The sampler. . . . Did you get it framed?"

"It's at the frame shop. My mom is supposed to stop by and get it before coming in later today. Would you like to have it back?"

She shook her head. "No. I think you had a lovely idea of making it sort of a memorial to Grandma and my great-great-grandmother. Cary did bring you the genealogical information on them, didn't he?"

"He did," I said, "and I'm working on the narrative. I should have it finished in another day or so."

She stood and handed me a business card. "Please let me know when the display is ready. I'd love to see it."

"I will, Eleanor."

She left then, turning at the door to wave good-bye. I swallowed the lump in my throat and felt guilty that I'd thought Eleanor was interested only in her grandmother's money.

The ringing of the phone snapped me out of my reverie. It was Mom.

"Hello, darling," she said. "Angus and I have had a lovely breakfast of eggs, bacon, toast, and strawberries. Then we felt simply terrible thinking about you there, probably having had nothing for breakfast yourself, and we thought I should call and ask if you'd like anything."

I laughed. "No, thank you. Please tell Angus I appreciate his concern and thoughtfulness, and, of course, I appreciate yours, too, Mom. You could bring lunch when you come, though."

"I'll do that. See you about eleven thirty or twelve."

"Say, Mom, you'll never believe who came in this morning."

"Was it Dreadful Devon?" she asked.

"No, it was Eleanor Ralston. And she was completely different from the way she was at the funeral home. She asked that I call her when I get the display done."

"Really? After so thoroughly giving you the brush-off the other night?"

"Yeah. Maybe she was just overwrought then."

"Maybe," Mom said, although she didn't sound convinced.

"Anyway, I have a flash drive on my desk in the office . . . just to the right of the mouse. It has the narrative of the history of samplers and the information about Louisa Ralston and her great-grandmother on it. I thought I might try to finish it before class."

"All right. I'll slip the flash drive into my purse when I go upstairs to get dressed."

"Thanks, Mom. See you soon."

"Any special requests for lunch?" she asked.

"Nah, you know what I like."

As we ended our conversation, a customer came in. She bought knitting needles and four skeins of white yarn. Seriously, white yarn was hot. I definitely needed to have a talk with Riley.

During the midmorning lull, I sat in the sit-

and-stitch square and worked on Riley's burp cloth. It was peaceful to let everything drift out of my mind except counting and stitching. This was a cross-stitch piece, and the border was so sweet and dainty. It was going quickly, too. I figured I'd be done with it within the next day or so.

The bells above the shop door jingled. I looked up and saw Devon Reed entering with a bouquet of daisies.

"I know I was supposed to call first," he said, "but I was in the neighborhood." He held out the flowers. "These are for you. They're a peace offering."

"Thank you." I put my work on the ottoman and went to accept the flowers. "That wasn't necessary, but I gratefully accept. If you give me a second, I'll just get a vase for these." I stepped into my office and retrieved a vase, then filled it a third of the way with water from the bathroom. I cut the stems diagonally and arranged them in the vase.

"There," I said, setting the flowers on the counter. "They look like a glimpse of spring sitting there, don't they?"

"They do," Devon said. "I'm glad you like them. I take it Mumsy and the hound are elsewhere this morning?"

"Yes, they are. So, let's talk." I returned to my red chair, and Devon took a seat on one of the navy sofas.

"The freelance business hasn't been too kind to me so far," he said. "I haven't been at it all that long, and I feel a hard-hitting story is exactly what I need to get my career off the ground."

"Well, you must have had a lucrative career prior to embarking upon your freelancing gig," I said, looking pointedly out the window at his car.

"I did. I was a stockbroker in Seattle. But the job stress got to be too much to handle, and I decided to follow my heart and do something completely different. You can understand that, can't you?"

"I can. I did the very same thing."

Devon leaned forward. "That's why I want to investigate Louisa Ralston's murder. The sensational story of the little old lady who was murdered in a small town. It could be not only national newspaper or magazine fodder, but it could even get me on TV."

"Devon, I don't think it's right to exploit a woman's murder and her family's grief merely to get your fifteen minutes of fame."

"That's not what I'm doing," he said.

I arched a brow.

"Okay, it's a *little* of what I'm doing," he said. "But mainly I'm bringing justice to Louisa Ralston and her family. Marcy, come on. The woman died in your store. Don't you want to know why?"

"Of course, I do, but —"

"Then help me find out. You know people in this town. They'll talk to you." He propped his elbows on his knees. "I'll let you share the byline, if that's what you want."

"I don't care about sharing the byline," I said. "And I don't know as many people in this town as you seem to think. I haven't been here all that long myself."

He sat back and sighed. "Then you won't help me?"

"I'll help you . . . but only because I want Louisa Ralston's killer brought to justice." I still didn't trust him as far as I could throw him, but if he found out something about Louisa Ralston or her murder, I wanted him to let me in on whatever it was.

He grinned. "Terrific. Hey, maybe Reese Witherspoon will play you in the movie."

I rolled my eyes. "Sure. It's the role she's been waiting for."

"How about we get that interview knocked out while I'm here?" Devon asked, taking his recorder from his coat pocket. "I don't want my editor to think I've completely forgotten him."

"Let's do it."

Devon flipped the recorder on. He repeated his bit about being Devon Reed and interviewing me as the entrepreneur of the Seven-Year Stitch. He then asked me how long I'd been in business. I told him, and he moved on to, "What did you do prior to opening your business, Marcy?"

"I was an accountant in San Francisco. When this space became available, my friend Sadie — she and her husband own MacKenzies' Mochas down the street — called me and convinced me to open my embroidery store."

"So you simply dropped everything and moved to Tallulah Falls?" Devon asked.

"Yeah . . . I guess basically that's what I did."

"No real roots in San Francisco, then, eh?"

"I'll always have roots in San Fran," I said. "It's still home in many ways. But every day, Tallulah Falls is becoming more of a home to me, too."

I'd no sooner finished that sentence than Mom and Angus came bursting through the front door. Devon paused the recorder. Angus bounded over to greet me and then gave Devon a curious sniff.

"He doesn't bite, does he?" Devon asked.

"No," I said. "He's a sweetheart."

"I wouldn't be too sure," Mom said.

I shot her a warning glance, and she gave me a saucy shrug.

"What's going on?" she asked, putting a large bag that I assumed contained the framed sampler behind the counter and a bag of heavenly-smelling takeout on the counter beside the daisies. "Did I miss anything?"

"Devon decided to come by and finish the interview," I said.

"Please continue," she said, coming over to sit in the vacant red chair. "Don't let Angus and me interrupt."

When Devon had concluded the interview, Mom made him replay the entire thing. "Just so I can see what I missed before I got here," she said. "This may be an exciting opportunity for my daughter, and I don't want to miss a single word."

Devon did replay the interview, and I had to admit it sounded good. If he did the interview based on the information he had, it would be solid reporting that might bring some new business into the Seven-Year Stitch.

"That was wonderful," Mom said. "Now what will you do? Have it transcribed, take notes, and write the article based on what Marcy has told you, or what? How does your process work, Devon?"

"I'll listen to the interview again and then write my article." He stood. "I really must be on my way. Marcy, let me get a photo of you sitting there where you are, and then we'll take one of you standing by the counter with your mom."

"Wait. Let me move to the sofa," I said. I wasn't dressed as nicely as I had been yesterday. Today I'd worn comfortable jeans, a waffle-knit kelly green henley, and sneakers, but I supposed it would have to do. Comfort comes before vanity on class days. "With this green shirt on, I'll look like a Christmas elf sitting in this red chair."

He laughed. "You've got a point." He snapped a photo of me on the sofa and then instructed me to stand in front of the counter. "Ms. Singer, stand over there with her so I can get you in the shot, too."

"Just take the picture of Marcy," Mom said. "It's her shop."

"Yeah, but it'll give the article heart for the two of you to be photographed together," he said.

"Come on, Mom," I said.

She heaved out a long sigh and then rose from the chair and joined me at the counter. I put my arm around her and tilted my head toward her. I smiled, she giggled, and that was when Devon took the photo.

"I'd like a copy of that," I said.

"I'll e-mail it to you. I'll let you know if I have any further questions. Thanks." With that, he turned and left.

Mom grabbed the bag of takeout — burgers, judging by the smell — and she and I wandered back to the sit-and-stitch square.

"The interview went well this time, don't you think?" I asked.

Mom didn't look up from her task of distributing the food among me, her, and Angus. "It was wonderful, love. But I still don't trust that man."

# Chapter Thirteen

After lunch, Mom minded the store while I went into the office and worked on the sampler history. I'd learned that the first known dated embroidery sampler was made in 1598 by a woman named Jane Bostocke. Jane had made the sampler to commemorate the birth of Alice Lee, presumed to be her daughter or niece. Today that sampler is part of a collection at the Victoria and Albert Museum. I included information about Jane's sampler and added the fact that samplers predated pattern books and traveled throughout Europe and the Middle East from person to person. The samplers were used to preserve information, as well as to teach the various stitches.

I then took out the information Cary had given me on Louisa and her great-grandmother. Louisa's great-grandmother had enjoyed a colorful — albeit hard — life. She'd come to Oregon as part of the Great

Migration of 1843. She was a fifteen-year-old bride. She and her husband had settled in the Willamette Valley, and he'd obtained work as a blacksmith.

Louisa came of age on the Oregon coast in the 1930s. She'd volunteered at the orphanage that would later become her home when she was seventeen. After that, she went to Seattle to study. She came back a couple years later, married Frank, and they later bought the orphanage and turned it into their private residence.

Fairly pleased with my narrative, I put a decorative floral border around the page and printed it out. I then took the piece to Mom to get an objective opinion. She was sitting at the counter, thumbing through her script and making notes, while Angus dozed in his bed at her feet.

"Would you read this and tell me what you think?" I asked.

"I'll be happy to." She perused the page and then looked up at me. "Sounds great. It does make me wonder what her great-grandma's original verse was."

"Me, too. And I wonder why Louisa tore it out."

"I guess we'll never know . . . unless someone saw the piece before Louisa took the seam ripper to it."

I nodded at her script. "How's that coming?"

"It's coming along fabulously," she said, grinning broadly. "It's a period piece set in midcentury Louisiana, and as I read through the script I can almost feel the lush fabrics I'll be working with. It's going to be so much fun. I've already spoken with Rob, the director, and we share the same vision on it . . . which makes things a lot easier when I'm planning out my costumes, jewelry, accessories, shoes. . . ."

I smiled. "It's nice to see you like this. I've missed seeing you get all excited over a new project and then go through your various stages of loving it, then hating it, then loving it, then —"

She tapped me on the arm with her pen. "Then come home. We can replicate this charming shop, you can have your own house. . . . You can get a fresh start away from memories of Timothy Enright and Louisa Ralston . . . away from people like Devon Reed. You know the shop would be just as successful in San Francisco as it is here — maybe even more successful."

I hugged her. "Thanks for the offer, Mom, but I live here now. I have a mortgage and a lease agreement."

"We can sell the house and sublet this space."

"I know, but I don't want to . . . not yet, anyway. I'm making a life for myself here, and I like it. I miss you, of course, and Frances and Alfred, too. But you're gone so much of the time, I get to see you more during your visits here than I ever did when I lived at home."

"Is it David?" she asked. "Are you afraid you'll run into him again and be reminded of the dreadful way he treated you?"

"No. I'm over David. Completely. I think he did me a favor by calling off our engagement at the last minute," I said. "Can you imagine how horrible it would've been had he gone ahead and married me? We'd have both been miserable, and we'd have already been divorced by now."

"I've just always worried it was David who drove you away from San Francisco."

"It wasn't. It was actually Sadie pulling me to Tallulah Falls rather than anyone driving me out of San Fran." I laughed. "It's all right for me to grow up, Mom. I'll be okay."

She leaned her head against my shoulder. "I know, darling. It's hard to let go, though. You'll see that one day when you have a daughter or son and want to protect that child from everything in the world. . . . And when you can't, you'll feel so helpless."

I kissed her cheek. "I love you, too."

Cary was the first person to show up for needlepoint class. "Am I on time?" he asked. "I've not missed anything, have I?"

"No," I said. "You're actually about half an hour early. But that's good. I can show you Louisa's sampler and the narrative I've laminated and placed on the wall next to it."

"Fantastic!" he said, turning that movie star smile on me.

"You know, you really are reminiscent of Cary Grant when he was young," I said.

"Truly," Mom said, from the sofa in the sit-and-stitch square.

"Thank you both," Cary said. "Let me share one of my favorite Cary Grant anecdotes with you. There was once a reporter who wired Grant's agent asking, 'How old Cary Grant?' Grant intercepted the message and wired back, 'Old Cary Grant fine. How you?' "

We laughed.

I said, "I read that Hitchcock once said Grant was the only actor he'd ever loved."

"Yes," Mom said, "I read that somewhere, too. I adored Grant and Kelly in *To Catch a Thief.*" She sighed. "Edith Head was nominated for an Oscar for her costume design in that movie."

"That's right. And what about *Roman Holiday* with Hepburn and Peck? Didn't she win for that one?" Cary asked.

"Yes, she did. She won eight Academy Awards in all and garnered a star on Hollywood's Walk of Fame."

"Oh, Mom, you'll get your star and your Oscar one of these days," I said.

"I'd better hurry, if I'm going to make it before I die."

"Nonsense," Cary said. "You're far too young to be so morbid, Ms. Singer. How about showing me that sampler?"

"It's right over here." I led him to the wall where I'd hung the sampler. "By the way, your cousin, Eleanor, was in this morning. I told her I'd let her know when I had the framed sampler on display. I'll have to call her later."

"Eleanor was here?" Cary asked. "That's odd. Did she say why she came?"

"She wanted to see where her grandmother died and to ask me if she'd had any last words," I said.

"And what did you tell her?"

I repeated to Cary what I'd told Eleanor earlier. "Before she left, she said she'd like to see the sampler once I had it framed."

Cary was frowning when I'd finished speaking. "Did I say something to upset you, Cary?"

"No, no, *ma belle.* I'm just confused about Eleanor's attitude. The Eleanor you saw at the funeral home the other night was the Eleanor we all know and love. Whoever this is who came into your shop wasn't Eleanor." He rubbed his chin thoughtfully. "Unless she's on some sort of medication or something. I'm sure the will had to be rather disappointing to her. Maybe the doc had to give her some happy pills."

"She said she received the house and its contents," I said. "I would think she'd be thrilled."

"She did get the house and furnishings, but she didn't get any money. Several of us family members received modest disbursements, but the majority of Aunt Louisa's estate went to some charity none of us had ever heard of." He shrugged. "Of course, Eleanor plans to sell the house and furnishings, so she'll have plenty of money to do with as she wishes."

I merely nodded, not quite knowing what to say.

Cary turned and spotted the sampler and laminated narrative on the wall. "Oh, this is lovely! What a wonderful homage to Aunt

Louisa and dear old Millie. You've outdone yourself, Marcy. On behalf of the Ralston family, I thank you."

"You're quite welcome," I said. "I'm glad you're happy with it."

At that point, Reggie Singh and Ella Redmond came in.

"Hey, there," Reggie said. She settled into one of the red chairs by Mom. "How are you this evening, Ms. Singer? Are you planning to stitch with us?"

"Nope. No stitching for me until I go back to work. I'm content to watch and chat," Mom said. "And please call me Beverly."

"What's so interesting?" Ella asked me and Cary.

"I framed the sampler Cary's Aunt Louisa and her great-grandmother Millicent Connor made," I said.

Ella and Reggie came over to look at the piece.

"This is exquisite," Reggie said. "Look at all those tiny stitches. And there's hardly any fading at all."

"It's been well preserved," I said.

"Did you say the piece was done by both Mrs. Ralston and her great-grandmother? They worked on it together?" Ella asked.

"Not exactly," I said. "Mrs. Ralston brought it into my shop. It's her great-grandmother's original, but I have reason to believe Mrs. Ralston tore out the verse initially on the sampler and replaced it with this one . . . which is actually a quote from *The Strange Case of Dr. Jekyll and Mr. Hyde.*"

"That's unusual," Ella said. "Don't you think?"

"I do think it's unusual," I said. "I was saying to Mom earlier today I'd love to know what the original verse said."

"I'll check with my mother and see if she knows anything about it," Cary said. "These days she remembers things from far in the past better than she can recall what she had for lunch. Perhaps she'll know something of interest about the original."

After everyone in the needlepoint class had arrived and had admired the sampler, we got to work. Cary had never done any type of needlecraft before, and I half suspected he was here only to visit with Mom. He and I chose an easy but attractive and manly pattern — a lion — for him, and he sat on the sofa beside Mom. I showed him how to get started, and Mom assured me she'd help him if he got stuck. Although Mom wasn't working on a project, she could do just about any type of embroidery if she wanted to, so I felt Cary was in good hands. I wondered if she might like him a little, too.

"Pretty daisies," Ella commented as she was threading her needle. "Do you have an admirer?"

"Not really. They're from a reporter who is doing an article about Tallulah Falls entrepreneurs," I said.

"I'd call him anything *but* an admirer," Mom said. "He was rather insulting when he first came in here and started interviewing Marcy."

"He was," I agreed. "But he said the flowers were a peace offering."

"Shabby peace offering," Cary said. "Don't get me wrong — they're very nice — but if I were to make a peace offering, I'd bring roses."

I grinned. "Yes, I do believe you would."

"So, how was the reporter insulting?" Reggie asked.

"He started asking questions about . . . about things that have gone wrong here in the shop," I said. "You know, the . . . um . . . uncomfortable situation with Mr. Enright . . . things like that." I didn't dare mention Devon's interest in Mrs. Ralston's death with her nephew sitting there.

"I'm not even convinced he's a real reporter," Mom said.

"You aren't?" Ella asked. "Why would a

fake reporter be interested in Tallulah Falls entrepreneurs?"

"I don't know," Mom said, "but an Internet search didn't turn up any articles by anyone bearing his name. I don't trust him."

"He said he was fairly new to freelancing," I said, not so much defending Devon as trying to keep my class from thinking I was an idiot for not vetting him properly before agreeing to grant him an interview.

"I think you're wise not to trust him, Beverly," Reggie said. "Through Manu's work, I've seen that people aren't always who or what they claim to be, and you never know what they might be up to. It pays to be cautious."

Reggie's comments tumbled around in my head as I worked on my needlepoint project — a pair of white orchids. What did I know about Devon Reed? Nothing other than what he'd told me. Was he really interested in arriving at the truth about Louisa Ralston, or would he sell me — and anyone else — out for the story that would bring him national coverage?

Cary's comments were interesting, too. What charity had Louisa Ralston donated her fortune to? Maybe I should go by and see Adam Gray before work tomorrow morning.

# Chapter Fourteen

Once again, I left Mom and Angus snoozing while I attended to business. I didn't mind, and since it was another class night — this time crewel — I knew it would do Mom good to sleep in. Actually, it would have done me good to sleep in, too. Mom and I had stayed up until after midnight last night talking . . . reminiscing . . . giggling.

It was really cold out this morning. I shivered as I cranked up the heater in the Jeep. Naturally, it blew out cold air because the engine wasn't warm yet. It warmed up just about the time I reached Adam Gray's office.

Mr. Gray had a small office in a strip of older buildings on First Street. His name was written in white Old English lettering on the front of his glass door. I opened the door and stepped inside.

"Good morning," said a receptionist to

my right. Her voice was so soft I could barely hear her. She looked thin, pale, and timid, and she had unruly copper curls hanging about her face. She suited Mr. Gray perfectly.

"Good morning," I said. "Is Mr. Gray available? I'm Marcy Singer, and I'd love to speak with him for just about five minutes if he has it to spare."

"I'll check with him and see." She picked up the phone and punched in an extension for Mr. Gray. She announced my arrival, said, "Okay," hung up, and turned to me. "He asked me to send you back. Go down this hallway. Mr. Gray's office is on the left."

I thanked her and sought out Mr. Gray. His office door was open, and I saw him sitting behind his desk before he caught sight of me. He looked positively engulfed in paper . . . in his suit . . . in this large office. He looked like a child playing lawyer rather than an actual lawyer. Or he would have if he hadn't looked so very old and tired. He appeared to have aged even since I'd seen him last.

"Mr. Gray, thank you for seeing me," I said as I walked into the office.

"You're quite welcome," he said. "Sit down. Tell me how I can help you."

I sat in one of the round-backed leather

chairs situated in front of his desk. "I promise I'll make this quick."

"Take your time. My first client isn't due for an hour."

I explained the Devon Reed situation to him. "Like Mr. Reed, I do want to know what happened to Mrs. Ralston, and if she was murdered, I want her killer brought to justice. But I don't feel it's right for him to sensationalize her death in order to make a name for himself."

"No, Marcy, neither do I. Besides, the police department is handling the matter. They don't need some Truman Capote wannabe doing their jobs for them."

"I agree." I looked down at the scuffed hardwood floor. "How *is* the investigation going?"

"Well, I've told them it's perfectly ridiculous for them to consider you a suspect," he said.

"But I still am one?"

He nodded. "I'm afraid so . . . at least for now. But don't worry. The truth will come to light."

"I know moments ago I criticized Devon Reed for hurrying the investigation along for his own benefit," I said, "but is there anything I can do to help the investigation along?"

"You're not doing the same thing as Devon Reed," he said with a consoling smile. "You're trying to clear yourself of suspicion of murder, and you're not planning to write some sort of tell-all about your experiences . . . unless I'm much mistaken." He chuckled, and I laughed, too.

"That said," he continued, "I do believe it's best to leave the detecting to the detectives."

"All right," I said. "I'll do that. By the way, Eleanor came to see me at the shop yesterday."

"Did she?"

"Yeah. She wanted to see the sampler her great-great-grandmother — or would that be great-great-great-grandmother?"

"Ms. Connor," Mr. Gray said.

I smiled. "Yes. She wanted to see it. Unfortunately, my mom hadn't picked it up from the framers yet, so she didn't get to look at it yesterday. I plan on calling her today to tell her to come back by when she gets a chance."

"Did it turn out well?" he asked.

"Very well. It looks wonderful. You should come by and see it when you have time."

"I'll do that. It's strange that Eleanor would stop in out of the blue," he said. "Did she ask for the sampler to be returned?"

"No. She said she thought it was a nice idea to display it in the shop with the brief history of samplers and the narrative about her relatives."

He steepled his fingers. "Yes, well, I imagine she asked around and found out that since the original was tampered with, it doesn't have much monetary value."

"You know, Cary also said her stopping by and acting nice was out of character," I said. "He was at the needlepoint class yesterday evening. He said Eleanor was disappointed with her settlement and that maybe the doctor had her on some sort of happy pills."

Mr. Gray chuckled again. "If anyone needs happy pills, it's Eleanor."

I shrugged. "She was really nice to me yesterday and didn't seem at all disappointed. She said she got the house and its contents."

"She did," Mr. Gray said. "Be sure to bring your mom to the auction on Saturday."

"I'm supposed to work on Saturday, but I suppose I could come before work. What time does the auction start?"

"It begins at nine a.m. Louisa had some lovely things I believe might interest you."

"Did she have an umbrella stand?" I

asked. "That's what I realize I need every time someone comes in and props an umbrella in the corner of the Seven-Year Stitch."

"As a matter of fact, she did. She had a lovely nineteenth-century cast-iron umbrella stand." He smiled. "If you're interested, though, bring a young man — maybe two — with you. That thing weighs a ton."

I laughed. "I'll keep that in mind. One other thing, Mr. Gray — do you by any chance know what the original verse on the sampler was? Or why Mrs. Ralston tore it out and replaced it with one from *The Strange Case of Dr. Jekyll and Mr. Hyde*?"

"Not a clue," he said. "In fact, the first time I'd ever seen that sampler was the day you brought it to Louisa's house." His face took on a wistful look. "Louisa could be private about some things. I don't think even Frank knew her as well as he thought he did."

"I've taken up enough of your time," I said. "Do stop by when you have a chance so you can see the sampler. I think you'll be pleased with the narrative I worked up about Mrs. Ralston, too."

"I'll see you soon," he said.

Before going on to work, I stopped at MacKenzies' Mochas. Blake was manning the counter while Sadie was serving some customers at a table in the back. Both of them were wearing red. Blake had on a red turtleneck and jeans. Sadie was wearing a red sweater dress with black ballerina flats.

"It's still January, right?" I asked.

"As far as I know," Blake said. "Why?"

"You guys look like you're dressed for Valentine's Day."

He grinned. "Yeah, I guess we are. We didn't plan it that way, but we thought it was pretty cool and decided neither of us should change."

"Aw, ain't love grand?" I laughed.

"Yep, it is. Speaking of which . . ." He nodded toward the door.

I turned to see Todd walk in.

"You guys talking about me?" he asked.

"Nope," I said. "I was asking Romeo here why he and Juliet are dressed like valentines."

Sadie arrived at the counter in time to hear my comment. "Because every day is St. Valentine's Day when you're with the one you love." She gave Blake a peck on the cheek.

That was an excellent sign. I hadn't seen Blake and Sadie this happy in weeks.

"So what's up with *you* this morning, Blue Bell?" she asked.

It was true. I was wearing a blue cowl-neck sweater that threatened to swallow me up. I love oversized sweaters on cold days.

"I came to see if any of you would like to go with me to an auction on Saturday," I said. "Sadie mainly, but you guys, too, of course."

"Of course," Blake said. "I know how you enjoy our shopping trips together."

I laughed. "Seriously, it'll be fun."

"I'll pass," Blake said. "Someone needs to stay here and mind the store. I'll be here when you guys finish your bidding."

"To do our bidding?" Sadie asked.

"Maybe you can persuade me," he said. "We'll see."

Todd made gagging noises. "Where's the auction, and what are they selling?"

"The auction is at Louisa Ralston's house, and they're selling off all her stuff. Mr. Gray said they have an umbrella stand I might be able to use at the Seven-Year Stitch . . . if I'm the winning bidder." I gave Todd a sidelong glance. "He did say it's really heavy, though."

"Oh, I see what this is," Todd said. "I'm being invited along for my muscles." He feigned a hurt look. "I feel so used."

"Haven't I warned you about these two?" Blake asked. "They're wily."

"Come on, Todd," I said. "Will you go? Mrs. Ralston has — had — some gorgeous things. Mom will probably come along, and if she has her way about it, she'll buy so much she'll need to hire a moving van. You probably won't have to carry a thing."

"Well, that's fine. I'm being used for my muscles, and now you're saying you might not even want *them,*" Todd said.

"You'd better mind your p's and q's, Todd," Sadie said. "That Cary Grant guy has been hanging around Marcy's shop quite a bit lately." Sadie winked, encouraging me to go along with her joke.

"And he scoffed at the daisies Devon Reed brought me as a peace offering," I said.

"Indeed he did," Sadie said. "The gentleman said *he'd* have brought roses."

"What're you saying here?" Blake asked. "You saying Marce here has her eye on the old guy?"

"He isn't all that old," I said.

"And I don't think he's as interested in needlepoint as he'd have us believe," Sadie said.

"Me, either. There's definitely another reason he's making frequent visits to the Seven-Year Stitch," I said. Then I giggled. "And I call her 'Mom.' "

Sadie laughed, too. "I know. Isn't it great?

It's so obvious he's into her, and I think she likes him, too."

"They have so much in common," I said. "It isn't often you find a man outside of Hollywood who can talk knowledgeably about the world of costume design."

"Wouldn't it be something if your mom fell in love with this guy and moved to Tallulah Falls?" Blake asked.

"Um . . . yeah," I said, my smile fading. "That . . . that *would* be something."

After securing Todd's promise that he would go with me to the auction on Saturday, I walked slowly up the street to work. I thought it was fantastic that Mom had found someone here in Tallulah Falls with similar likes, and the fact that the someone was a handsome guy was even better. But I wasn't sure I was ready for her to settle down here in Oregon. I mean, her home was in San Francisco. She was closer to work there . . . although, granted, her work took her all over the country and occasionally the world.

I knew it was highly doubtful that she would even consider moving here, but I found the thought a teensy bit disturbing. If she moved here, it would be the same as if I were to move back to San Francisco. I wouldn't feel like I was maintaining my independence anymore.

I unlocked the shop door and went inside. I was being silly. I had let our jokes at the coffeehouse get in my head. I put my things behind the counter, hung up my coat in the office, and checked my phone messages. My only message was from Mom.

"Hi, darling. I won't be in until later this afternoon. Cary called and he's taking me to brunch and then on to his shop. We've decided to make a day of it. I'll have my cell on if you should need me. Angus is in the backyard enjoying a rawhide bone."

# Chapter Fifteen

I was putting the finishing touches on Riley's burp cloth when Nellie Davis, owner of the aromatherapy shop two stores down, sashayed into the Seven-Year Stitch. Her short gray-and-white-streaked hair was sticking out all over the place. With her thick-framed red eyeglasses and her overly thin shape dressed in head-to-toe black, she looked a little comical standing there with her arms akimbo.

"Good morning, Ms. Davis," I said, suppressing a groan. The woman had never darkened my door other than to complain about something. "Is there something I can do for you?"

"Um . . . yes . . . yes, I think there is. I'd like some pink, white, and wine yarn. A skein of each should do it, I believe. I'm making a scarf."

Dumbfounded, I had to take a second before my brain could process what she'd actually said. "You want some yarn?"

"Yes," she said with a huff. "Pink, white, and wine, if you have it."

I put the burp cloth on the ottoman and got up to assist Ms. Davis. "Do you have a particular type of yarn in mind? Angora, wool, cotton . . . ?"

"Is . . . Is that where it happened?" she asked. "Over there near the sofa? I mean, I imagine she'd have asked to sit down."

"You imagine who would have asked to sit down, Ms. Davis?" I knew exactly who she meant — and now the real reason for her visit to the shop — but I decided to be obtuse. "Do *you* need to sit down? You do look a tad unwell."

"I'm fine," she snapped. "I was wondering where Louisa Ralston collapsed."

"It was here . . . in the store," I said, my eyes wide with feigned innocence.

"I know that." She smirked. "In fact, I told that handsome reporter who came to ask me questions about running a business in Tallulah Falls that Louisa Ralston wasn't the first person to die in your store."

"Mrs. Ralston didn't die in my store."

"She might as well have. Timothy Enright did."

"I don't see how any of this concerns you, Ms. Davis."

"It concerns me because I own a shop on this street. I don't want people to stop shopping here because your embroidery store is cursed or something."

I spoke through gritted teeth. "My shop is not cursed."

The bells over the shop door jingled, and I turned to see Devon Reed stride in, looking relaxed and carefree in tan slacks and brown pullover.

"Good morning, ladies," he said. "Ms. Davis, you're looking well."

She smiled up at him. "Thank you, Mr. Reed. You're looking nice yourself. I was trying to discuss my concerns with Marcy here, but she doesn't seem to care that her shop might run the rest of us out of business."

"Ms. Davis," I said, "my shop is doing well. Business is booming. If yours isn't and you feel your customers are being driven away, you might want to look for something to blame other than my shop."

"Yes, well, I need to get back," she said. "I left a trusted customer in charge of the shop, and I don't want to inconvenience her any longer."

I didn't ask her about the yarn she'd been looking for. I'd already realized it was merely an excuse to come in and that she didn't actually want it, anyway.

As soon as she left, I turned on Devon. "So *that's* where you got your information about Timothy Enright and Louisa Ralston?" I asked. "That old busybody?"

"No. I talked to you before talking to her, if you'll recall. Besides, I did my homework on all of you before I set up interviews," he said. "She was, however, more than happy to supply additional details about you, your shop, and the murderous happenings at the 'Stitch.' "

"What could she possibly know about me?" I asked. "Before today, I'd spoken with her only one other time."

"She told me you left San Francisco after being jilted by the love of your life. Neither you nor your mother is able to untie the apron strings just yet, even though you're well into your thirties." He gave me a snarky smile. "Shall I continue?"

"No, you most certainly shall not," I said. "How does she know so much about me? And why does she care?"

"She knows so much about you because this is a gossipy little town." He spread his hands. "I'm not sure *care* is the proper word to express how she feels. Maybe she's concerned that your reputation for having people die in your store will scare away aromatherapy customers."

"I'd like to scare *her* away," I said.

He wandered over to the sofa and sat down. I resumed my seat on the red chair and picked up the burp cloth.

"I was driving through town this morning looking for some breakfast and saw your Jeep parked outside Adam Gray's office," Devon said. "Have you learned anything new?"

"No, I haven't." I was angry with Devon, angry with Ms. Davis, and angry with myself. I wished I was able to trust Devon, to have him help me figure out who killed Mrs. Ralston so that once again suspicion for a crime I did not commit would be off my shoulders. But I couldn't trust him. He was a stranger and a sensationalist who seemed to want his fifteen minutes of fame, no matter what cost to anyone else.

"You seem engrossed in your work this morning," Devon said. "It's either that or you're upset with me about something. Did dear old Mumsy not like the interview?"

"No, Devon, she thought it was fine. I'm doing this for a client, and I'd like to get it finished up, that's all." I glanced up at him. "Plus, I don't think I'm the right person to help you figure out what happened to Mrs. Ralston. Since Ms. Davis is so well connected and informed, maybe the two of you can solve the crime, be the heroes, and write the book."

"I don't know why you're getting so huffy with me." He stood. "Call me if you get in a better mood." He stormed out the door.

I thought about yelling after him that the daisies were a pathetic peace offering, but I didn't want to be childish. Besides, I liked the daisies. It was their giver I didn't particularly care for.

A customer came in excited that her granddaughter had asked her to tutor her in embroidery. The woman looked young to be a grandmother, and she reminded me somewhat of Mom.

"I'm going to start her out with some redwork," she said. "Do you have any iron-on designs?"

I smiled, glad for the more pleasant company. "I certainly do." I led the woman back to where the pattern books, kits, and iron-on design packets were located. "What is she into? Horses, unicorns, fairies, butterflies . . . ?"

The woman laughed. "All of the above!"

"Well, you pick out your design," I said, "and I'll go round up some red embroidery floss."

"Thank you."

She wound up settling on two design packets. One had butterflies and flowers; the other had unicorns and winged horses.

"She'll love these," I said, as I rang up her design packets and five skeins of red floss.

"I think she will, too."

I handed her a flyer. "If the two of you would ever like to take a class together here at the Seven-Year Stitch, I offer classes on Tuesdays, Wednesdays, and Thursdays."

"I'll keep that in mind." She tucked the flyer into the periwinkle bag with her purchases before leaving the shop.

I had just deflated back onto the red chair in a renewed bout of self-pity when Ted Nash arrived, looking business-casual in his dark blue suit and blue-and-white pinstriped shirt open at the collar.

"You okay?" he asked.

"I guess." I sighed. "No, I'm actually not all right. That reporter who did the entrepreneur interviews wants me to help him discover who killed Louisa Ralston. Even though I'd love to find out who *did* kill Mrs. Ralston, I don't want to share information with him. I don't trust him."

"Follow your instincts on that one," Ted said. "I don't trust him, either, and I've never even met the guy. I can tell there's something more, though. What else is eat-ing you?" He took a seat on the navy sofa.

"It's Mom. She went to brunch with Cary Ellis today. He's Louisa Ralston's nephew."

"The one taking the needlepoint class?"

"Yeah," I said. "How did you know?"

"Sadie was talking about him with Blake this morning when I was buying coffee."

"What was she saying?"

Ted shrugged. "Only that he's taking the class and he seems to really like your mother."

"That's what bothers me," I said. "Mom barely knows this man!"

He chuckled. "A little role reversal going on here? Some *Freaky Friday* on a Wednesday?"

"It's more than that," I said. "Her life is in San Francisco."

"And if she decides to make a life for herself here, she steps all over your toes, right?"

I bit my lower lip.

"It's okay," he said. "I'm not going to tell her. You *can* confide in me, you know."

"I do know, Ted. Thank you." I sighed again. "And I know I'm overreacting. I love Mom, but I don't want to be in her shadow anymore. I lived in her shadow my entire life until I came here. Tallulah Falls is mine. I'm making my own friends, I bought my own house, and I bought my own furniture." I frowned. "Does that make any sense?"

"It makes perfect sense."

"Maybe. But it still makes me feel like a selfish jerk," I said. "This case has me a jittery mess."

He smiled. "You aren't a selfish jerk. And here's another thing — you don't need Devon Reed to help you figure out what happened to Louisa Ralston."

"I know, I know," I said. "The Tallulah County Police Department is working on it."

"They're not the only ones. I'm working on it, too, when I have the time . . . mostly on my own time."

"Really?" My eyes watered a little. "Thank you."

"Don't thank me yet," he said. "I haven't been able to turn up very much, and you are still a suspect. But I did find this out."

Before he could finish that thought, the two detectives from the Tallulah County Police Department — Detectives Bailey and Ray — burst into the shop. They were both wearing tweed sport coats, and I immediately thought, *Oh, super. It's Tweedledee and Tweedledum.*

"Ms. Singer," Detective Bailey said, "we need to speak with you privately."

I tentatively got to my feet, my eyes pleading with Ted to do something.

"I'm Detective Ted Nash of the Tallulah Falls Police Department." Ted stood and took out his badge to show to the other two officers. "What's this about?"

"This doesn't concern you, Detective Nash," Detective Bailey said. "If you're questioning Ms. Singer about another matter, we'll wait our turn."

"I'm not here at the moment as a representative of the department," Ted said. "But as a professional courtesy, I would appreciate your telling me what this is about."

"All right," Detective Bailey said, hooking his thumbs through his belt loops. "Adam Gray had a heart attack in his office this morning."

I gasped. "Poor Mr. Gray. . . . But I saw him earlier, and he appeared to be fine."

"We know you saw him earlier," Detective Ray said, nodding. "That's why we're here." He took a notebook from his breast pocket and flipped it open. "The secretary — a Ms. Sherman — said you arrived at the office just after they opened. She said you had no appointment but insisted on seeing Mr. Gray."

"I don't think I *insisted,*" I said. "I requested to see him, and he agreed, since his first appointment wasn't due to arrive for an hour."

"What did the two of you speak about?" Detective Bailey asked.

"I went into his office and screamed, 'Boo,' to make him have a heart attack," I said. "Is that your ridiculous assumption?"

Ted leaned closer to me. "Marcy, don't antagonize them," he whispered.

To my horror, my eyes filled with tears. "I told Mr. Gray about that reporter Devon Reed and his intention to exploit Mrs. Ralston's murder for his own gain." The tears overflowed and rolled down my face. "And he told me about the auction."

Ted took a packet of tissues from his pocket, opened it, and handed me one.

"Thanks." I dried my eyes and sniffled. "I feel terrible about Mr. Gray. He really did seem to be all right when I was there. I didn't notice anything out of the ordinary."

"Did he eat or drink anything in your presence?" Detective Ray asked. "And be honest — Ms. Sherman will be asked to corroborate."

"No," I said. "He didn't have so much as a cup of coffee — at least, not that I saw. Did he have a heart condition?"

"We're looking into that," Detective Ray said. "We're also requesting that the coroner look specifically for Halumet while she's doing the autopsy."

I frowned. "Then you think the same person who murdered Mrs. Ralston might have murdered Mr. Gray?"

"It appears that may be the case," Detective Bailey said. "Did you retain any of the Halumet confiscated from your home, Ms. Singer?"

"No, I did not. I wasn't even aware there was Halumet in my home until your officers discovered it. The bottle has been in your possession ever since," I said.

"That's all the questions we have for now," Detective Bailey said.

Detective Ray flipped the notebook closed and returned it to his pocket. "Don't leave town."

As they left, I slumped against Ted. "Can this get any worse?" I asked.

"Never ask that," he said. "When you ask that question, things invariably get worse."

# Chapter Sixteen

I closed the shop at five p.m. to go home, eat dinner, and feed Angus. There was no indication Mom had been home at all today, and another call to her cell phone went straight to voice mail.

I heated a mug of soup in the microwave while I fed Angus. While I ate my soup and crackers, I allowed him to stay in the backyard. Before going back to work, I took him for a walk through the neighborhood. On my way back to the house, I spotted a patrol car. The officer gave me a friendly nod, and I realized Ted had likely asked the officers on patrol in this area to keep an eye on things here. I was glad for the extra security and made a mental note to thank Ted.

I felt weird about Mr. Gray. I was saddened by his sudden death, of course, but the fact that he'd suffered a heart attack freaked me out on more than one level. First off, if Mr. Gray had somehow ingested Halumet, it meant Mrs. Ralston's killer was at it again. Second, it meant I was also a suspect in *his* death. And last of all, it might mean that someone was trying to set me up.

I returned to the shop and began preparations for the class. I'd still had no word from Mom. Mom being Mom, I knew better than to worry, but that didn't stop the nagging doubt from tugging at the back of my mind telling me that something was wrong.

Tonight's crewel class had four members: Vera Langhorne, who was also in the needlepoint class; Julie and her daughter, Amber, who'd been in an earlier cross-stitch class; and April, a young woman who was painfully shy. I was hoping that expressing herself in class would be a way for her to learn to be more extroverted in other ways as well.

Julie and Amber were the first to arrive. I offered them something to drink — I always keep my mini-fridge well stocked, especially on class nights. They both chose a bottle of water. We made small talk — mostly about Amber's high school classes — until April arrived.

April mumbled a hello and went to the

red chair farthest from the group. She refused a drink and began unpacking her embroidery kit.

Vera swooped in, full of bluster and chatter. "Shoot, it's getting cold out there, girls. We'll need to wear our thermal underwear if it gets any colder." She smiled, taking off her coat and handing it to me so I could hang it in my office. "How is everybody tonight?"

The requisite *fines* and *okays* went up all around.

"You seem to be doing better than the rest of us put together," I said, returning from hanging up her coat. "What's got you so cheerful?"

Before she could answer, Mom breezed in. "Hi, everyone." She turned and waved good-bye to Cary, who then drove away. "Forgive me for being late. Did I miss anything?"

"Almost," Vera said. "I was just getting ready to ask everyone if they're planning to attend the Ralston estate auction on Saturday."

"I didn't know about it," Mom said. "Did you, Marcy?"

"I found out this morning," I said, declining to offer any further information until the two of us were alone.

"I wouldn't miss it," Vera said, sitting on the sofa facing the window. "All that luscious Victorian furniture . . . I might buy an entire set." She cocked her head. "I'm not sure I want to replace my comfy living room suite, but I'd love to get the winning bid on one of those bedroom ensembles." She clasped her hands. "Just thinking about it and how I'd redo the master bedroom makes me absolutely giddy."

I smiled. "I can see that. And here I am hoping to have the winning bid on an umbrella stand to go in the corner so customers will have a place to put their wet umbrellas while they shop."

Vera laughed. "Oh, Marcy, dear, you have to be more ambitious than that. What about a beveled mirror or an ornamental vase?"

"We'll see," I said.

"It sounds as if you've cased the place and made a list," Mom said jokingly.

"They ran an abbreviated item list in the paper this morning," Vera said. "There were a couple photographs, too." She frowned. "You don't think the auction house will postpone due to Adam Gray's death, do you?"

Mom's eyes widened and her jaw dropped. "Adam Gray died? When?"

"This morning," I said. "I tried to reach

you, but all my calls went to voice mail."

Mom held on to the counter for support as she went around and sat on the stool. "I feel positively light-headed. How did it happen?"

"Heart attack," Vera said. "Just like poor Louisa Ralston."

"Exactly like Mrs. Ralston," I said evenly.

"But what —" Mom began.

"We'll talk about it after class." I took my usual seat in the red chair, where I'd already spread my work out on the ottoman. "Did everyone do well this week? Any problems?"

No one had encountered any problems with the work, and they had all made good progress. Amber, especially, had a knack for needlecraft. Her design was two swans on a lake in springtime, and it was turning into a beautiful piece.

When the class was over and everyone had left, I busied myself by straightening up the shop. I dusted the coffee table, counter, and shelves, ran the electric sweeper over the floor, and sprayed fabric freshener on the sofas and chairs.

Mom still sat at the counter. "I'm sorry I wasn't available today."

"I just don't know why you had your calls going directly to voice mail," I said, not looking at her. "Didn't it occur to you that something might happen and that I might need you?"

"You seldom need me, Marcella. We're usually hundreds — if not thousands — of miles away from each other."

I tidied a stack of pattern books. "But you're here now. When you're here, I expect to be able to reach you."

She sighed. "I'm sorry. I was having fun."

"Goody for you, Mom. I was here getting accused of another murder."

"B-but you said Mr. Gray had a heart attack," she said.

"He did. But according to the officers who were here — you remember Detectives Ray and Bailey, don't you? — they specifically asked the coroner to check for Halumet. Why? you may ask. Because I was at Mr. Gray's office just a couple hours before he died."

"What were you doing there?" she asked.

"I went to let him know about Devon Reed and his hope to sensationalize Louisa Ralston's death for his own gain." I pushed my hair off my forehead. "And I went to try to get some insight into who might've killed Mrs. Ralston. I need to clear myself of any inkling of guilt associated with her death."

"But, darling, either way, they can't accuse you of Adam Gray's death. If there's no Halumet in his system, then he died of natural causes. If there *is* Halumet in his system, you're still absolved because they have the pills that were found in the nightstand."

"Except they can say they had no idea how many pills were in that bottle originally. And they can surmise that I must've kept some of them in order to carry out future nefarious schemes like killing Adam Gray."

Mom blew out a breath. "You're right. I should've been here today."

"No, it's me. It's been a rough day, that's all. Before I found out about Mr. Gray, the woman from the aromatherapy shop — Nellie Davis — came in and insinuated that I'm bad for business and that my shop is cursed because people keep dropping dead in it."

Mom got up and gave me a hug. "We'll get through this. Want me to throw a brick through the old lady's window?"

I grinned. "No. Yes . . . but no."

"At least that idea made you smile."

"Tell me about Cary's shop," I said.

"It's lovely," she said. "It's a classy little boutique with designer originals — both bigger names and people you've probably never heard of. At least not yet. And Cary employs students from the local design school in the shop to assist customers. They really know their stuff."

"Good. And you said on your message you were going to brunch?"

"That turned in to lunch, actually," she said. "Cary had a couple stops to make before he picked me up, so he was later than he'd expected to be."

"Would you like to go over to the Brew Crew and have a soda before we go home?" I asked.

"Sounds good."

We retrieved our coats from the rack in the office, locked up, and walked across the street to Todd's pub and craft brewery. I sometimes stop by after work when Angus isn't with me to get a soda and say hello before heading home. It helps me switch gears and get out of work mode and into home mode. Besides, it's always nice to see Todd.

The Brew Crew was crowded this evening, and Todd was busy. He made me a diet soda with vanilla and poured Mom a cup of decaffeinated coffee.

"Can't I cajole either of you into a beer this evening?" he asked.

"Not me," I said. "I'm driving."

"And I need to keep my head clear to help Marcy fend off the next wave of attacks,"

Mom said.

Todd frowned. "Wave of attacks?"

"Yeah. Nellie Davis came in today and accused me of scaring business away from Emerson Street," I said. "She says my shop is cursed because folks keep dying there."

"Yep, I see where she's coming from," Todd said, looking around his crowded pub. "This place is dead." He grinned. "Don't let her get to you. She's just old and lonely and weird."

"But that's not all," Mom said quietly. "Adam Gray had a heart attack today, and the Tallulah County detectives are trying to pin that on Marcella, too."

"What?" Todd asked.

I sighed and explained about their visit and the fact that they were having the coroner run tests for Halumet.

"I'm sorry." Todd looked around the bar. "I can get my assistant manager to cover for me, and we can —"

"Not necessary," I said. "I'm pretty tired, and I expect Mom is, too."

Mom nodded her agreement.

"So we'll probably turn in early," I continued. "Thank you for the offer, though."

"Well, if you guys need anything — if there's anything I can do to help — you know I will," Todd said.

"I know," I said. "And I appreciate it."

Mom and I finished our drinks. Todd was talking with another customer at the other end of the bar. I didn't want to leave without telling him good-bye, so I was watching to try to catch his eye and wave him over. Suddenly I caught sight of an auburn-haired woman.

I leaned over to Mom. "Isn't that Ella Redmond? She's in the needlepoint class and is the new genealogist at the library."

Mom squinted. "Yes, I believe that is her."

"Should I go over and say hello?" I asked.

"I suppose it wouldn't hurt," Mom said, "unless she's with someone. It might be awkward if she's on a date or something."

"No, of course I wouldn't want to intrude," I said. "Still, to be polite, we'll stop by her table and speak on the way out."

"All right."

I caught Todd's eye and waved good-bye. He held up a finger to let me know he wanted us to wait. He then came over and reiterated that he'd be happy to help us in any way. We said our good-byes and began weaving through the crowd toward Ella Redmond's table.

Before we got there, a man approached the table with a drink in each hand. The man was Devon Reed.

Ella looked up at Devon, smiled, and then noticed we were standing there. Her smile froze. "Marcy . . . and Ms. Singer . . . hello."

"Hi, there," I said. "We spotted you and wanted to say hello before we left. Hope you're having a nice evening."

"We are," Devon said with a smile. "And I hope you are, too."

"I wasn't aware you two knew each other," Mom said.

"We . . . we met at the library," Ella said.

"Oh, yeah. We reporters always have research to do," Devon said. "And knowing a genealogist always comes in handy."

"I guess it does," I said. "Well. See you guys later."

"Later, Marcy," Devon said.

"Wonder what's up with that," Mom said when we left the Brew Crew.

"I don't know," I said. "But I'm guessing it has something to do with Devon's research into Louisa Ralston's death."

# Chapter Seventeen

I didn't have to wait long to find out that I was right about Devon's being with Ella Redmond at the Brew Crew. He came into the shop Thursday just as I was opening up.

"Good morning," he said, looking around. "Where's your mom? Did she tie one on last night and have to stay home this morning to sleep it off?"

"No," I said coolly. "She had a manicure this morning. What can I do for you, Devon?"

"It's more what I can do for you," he said. "You're gonna thank me when I get you and your little store here out of hot water over Louisa Ralston's death."

"Well, if you can do that, I certainly will thank you."

"Good. I'm looking forward to it," he said. "So I had Ella Redmond look into Louisa Ralston's background. Before Louisa married Frank Ralston, she was a Connor. According to the information Ella was able to find, Louisa Connor and Edward Larkin announced their engagement in the newspaper in nineteen thirty-eight."

"You mean, Louisa was married once before?" I asked.

Devon shook his head. "The wedding never happened. The guy joined the military and left town."

"That's sad."

"It was apparently very sad for Louisa. After he left, she worked in the orphanage for two years."

"Did Ella learn what happened to Edward Larkin?" I asked.

"He went on about his life," Devon said. "He was honorably discharged from the army, and then he settled in the Midwest — Nebraska, I think she said. Had a family and lived a good long life until he had an accident one day on his way home from work."

"Poor Louisa," I said. "Wonder what happened."

Devon lifted his shoulders. "My guess is that he got cold feet. They were eighteen years old. Although back then lots of people settled down and started a family at that age, I'm not sure many of them knew what they were getting themselves into."

"Still, that's a lousy way to treat someone," I said.

"Spoken like a woman who's been there." Devon arched a brow.

I let his comment hang. I didn't owe him any explanations. "And you think all this information about Edward Larkin and Louise being jilted has something to do with her being murdered, oh, seventy years later?"

"I don't know," he said. "But it's something. If nothing else, it adds drama to her story when I *do* get all the pieces together." He rested his elbows on the counter. "Let's go out to dinner tonight and put our heads together — just you and me this time."

"I can't tonight," I said. "I have a class."

"All right. What about tomorrow, then?"

"I'll have to make sure Mom hasn't made plans," I said, hedging. Somehow it seemed rude to give him a flat-out no.

"Fine. I'll check with you tomorrow afternoon, and if you haven't made plans, we'll go to dinner. Is it a date?"

"Devon, I don't know anything about Louisa Ralston other than what I've told you," I said. "I don't know anything about anyone who might've wanted to do her in."

"But you can help me find out," he said.

"I'm not sure I *want* to help you find out."

"You'd rather have people think that your store is cursed? Or worse?"

"No, of course not, but —"

"I'll call you tomorrow afternoon," Devon said, heading for the door. "And I won't take *no* for an answer."

I looked down at Angus, who was dozing in his bed beneath the counter. "Some help you are. You could've growled at him and scared him away or something."

He wagged his tail.

Cary blew in at lunchtime carrying a vase of red roses in one hand and a picnic basket in the other. He was wearing brown trousers, a white polo shirt, and a tan sport coat. Naturally, I didn't say anything to Mom, but he was starting to creep me out with his obvious imitation of Cary Grant. Okay, so the man was his namesake. You don't see every woman named Marilyn — even if she *is,* in fact, named after Marilyn Monroe — dyeing her hair platinum, putting on a beige gown, and doing a breathless rendition of "Happy Birthday" to various and sundry presidents.

*I mean, come on — show some individuality, Cary!* That is, of course, what I *wanted* to say — not what I actually said. I actually said, "Hey, what a nice surprise!"

"Thank you, Marcy," he said. "Is your mom around?"

"She's walking Angus at the moment, but she'll be right back."

"Terrific. By the way, I spoke with my mother this morning, and she'd love to see Aunt Louisa's sampler."

"Can she come in to the shop?" I asked. "Or would you rather take it to her?"

"I'd rather take it to her," he said.

Mom stepped in as Cary said that. "Take what to whom?" she asked.

Angus immediately trotted over to sniff the picnic basket.

"Ah, now, this isn't for you, young man. Not entirely, anyway. I do have a ham bone in there for you if your mistress will allow you to have it." Cary looked at me.

"Sure," I said, "but could you hand it to me? I'll put it and Angus in the bathroom while we enjoy our picnic."

I took Angus and the bone into the bathroom, where Angus immediately sat down on the rug and went to work. I pulled the door shut and returned to the main part of the store, where Mom and Cary were busy arranging our picnic lunch on the coffee table.

"Cary tells me his mother would like to see the sampler," Mom said.

"Right," I said. "He's going to take it to her. Aren't you, Cary?"

"As a matter of fact, I'd like the three of us to take it to her. I thought that tomorrow afternoon when you close the shop, we could pick up some food and go have dinner with her." He smiled. "How does that sound?"

"It sounds lovely," Mom said.

"I'll feel rather like a third wheel," I said. "Wouldn't you two prefer to go alone?"

"Of course not," Cary said. "I want Mother to meet you both. You can always bring a date if that would make you feel better."

"I think I will, if you're sure you don't mind."

Mom grinned at me. "Todd?"

"Ted."

I called Ted as I was taking Angus home before class. Mom was staying at the shop, saying she was too full for dinner after the picnic lunch Cary had brought us. I said I'd bring us both a salad from home.

I had to admit, lunch had been nice. Cary had brought cucumber sandwiches, potato salad, green bean casserole, and coconut cream pie — all of which had been made by his mother's live-in cook — which made me wonder why we were picking up takeout for dinner tomorrow night, but I hadn't asked because I didn't want to appear rude.

Ted didn't answer until the third ring.

"Hi, it's Marcy. Am I interrupting anything?"

He expelled a breath. "No . . . not really. What's up?"

"It can wait," I said. "I can tell you're busy."

"I'm busy, but this actually concerns you. I would've phoned you in a few minutes, anyway. You must have ESP or something," he said.

"Okay." I drew out the word, wanting to know what he was talking about but dreading it at the same time.

"I got a copy of Adam Gray's toxicology report faxed to me from the Tallulah County PD a few minutes ago."

"Don't tell me," I said.

"Better me than someone else."

"They found Halumet, didn't they?"

"Yeah," he said. "They did."

"That was quick," I said.

"I know. They put a rush on it."

"So now what?"

"I'm not sure." He blew out another breath. "They'll either talk with you again, or they'll try to find more evidence before they do."

I groaned.

"Why did you call me?" he asked. "Is there something else going on?"

I explained about Cary and the trip to his mother's house for dinner tomorrow afternoon. "If it wouldn't interfere with your schedule and you wouldn't mind, I'd like you to go with me."

He laughed — and frankly, I found that a little insulting.

"A simple *no* would've sufficed," I said.

Still laughing, he said, "It's not that. I'd be happy to go. It's just that I've never been on a double date with a girl and her mother . . . and especially not to go meet her mother's boyfriend's *mother.*"

I started laughing, too. In fact, I laughed so hard, I had to pull off the road so I wouldn't wreck the Jeep. When I caught my breath, I said, "I hadn't even thought of it that way. It really is absurd, isn't it? We've been dumped into a Mel Brooks comedy." I started laughing again. "And the lead thinks he's Cary Grant."

Ted was still laughing, too. "What should I wear?"

"I'm wearing jeans and sneakers." I wiped the tears off my cheeks. "If we have to make an escape, I want to be able to run."

We hung up, and I took a tissue out of the glove box to further dry my cheeks and to remove the smudged mascara from under my eyes. That was a great laugh. I hadn't laughed that hard in who knew how long.

I only hoped I'd still be laughing when this entire mess was said and done. I was desperately hoping this visit to Cary's mother's house would be a way to learn more about Louisa Ralston, the replaced sampler verse, and whoever might have wanted to hurt either Louisa or Adam Gray. And having a detective of Ted's caliber there wouldn't hurt, either.

Besides, I wanted to get to know Ted better. Like me, Todd had been hurt before. In fact, Sadie and I'd had a huge argument when I found out she'd fixed me up with Todd even though she thought he was still hung up on Riley Kendall — yes, happily married, pregnant Riley. That had been three years ago, and now I believed Todd was over Riley, but I still felt I should proceed with caution. Of course, Ted was divorced, so I needed to be cautious there, too.

Was there any part of my life where I could throw caution to the wind? Even for just one day?

# CHAPTER EIGHTEEN

I returned to the shop an hour later, wearing fresh makeup and carrying two garden salads in plastic containers.

"These can't hold a candle to Cary's lunch," I said, "but then I don't have a live-in cook like his mom does. Or like you do, for that matter."

"Frances only comes in now on special occasions," she said.

"Since the Ellis cook can whip up food like she did today, then why did Cary say we'd stop for takeout on the way to his mother's house tomorrow?"

"I asked him that," Mom said, sitting on the sofa and opening her salad. "The cook is off on Fridays and Saturdays."

"Well, there you go." I went to my office and retrieved two diet sodas from the mini-fridge.

"Now I have a question for you," she said when I returned. "Why are you taking Ted rather than Todd to this dinner at Cary's house tomorrow evening?"

"Ted's being really great to me," I said, sitting on the sofa opposite her. "Even though this case isn't in his jurisdiction, he's helping me try to figure it all out. He's trying to protect me."

"And Todd?"

"I like Todd," I said, opening my own salad and trying to avoid Mom's prying eyes. "We've been out a few times, but I'm not looking for a serious relationship right now."

"Is he?"

"I don't know. Before Sadie introduced the two of us, he'd been involved pretty seriously with someone else."

"I remember your telling me about that," Mom said. "You and Sadie had quite an argument over it, didn't you?"

I nodded.

"What is she going to say about your asking Ted to dinner?"

"I don't know," I said. "But I can't worry about that right now. Todd has been through a rough breakup, Ted is divorced, and you know what I went through with David."

"Is that what this is really about?" she asked. "Are you afraid you'll get hurt again?"

"Partly. Maybe I am a bit gun-shy, but I don't want to get hurt, and I don't want to hurt someone else, either. I like both Todd and Ted, but I'm not sure I'm ready for an exclusive relationship with anyone at this point. And I'm not sure either of them is seeking a long-term commitment." I stabbed a chunk of lettuce. "I was so sure David was the one, Mom."

"I know you were, darling."

I sighed. "I guess that's how Mrs. Ralston must've felt about Edward Larkin."

"Who's Edward Larkin?" Mom asked.

"The guy Mrs. Ralston was engaged to before she met her husband, Frank." I looked up at Mom. "At least, that's the story Devon Reed was telling me this morning. He says Ella Redmond found that out for him."

"That confirms your theory on why the two of them were together at the Brew Crew last night."

I nodded. "Louisa's engagement to Edward was in the newspaper and everything. Then apparently Edward called off the wedding, left Oregon, and joined the army."

"How does Doofus Reed think any of that information will help him determine what happened to Mrs. Ralston?"

I giggled. "You remind me of Endora on

*Bewitched*."

"Gee, thanks."

"I don't mean it in a bad way," I said. "Remember how Endora used to call Darrin anything but Darrin? She usually called him Durwood." I frowned. "Wonder if she ever called *him* Doofus."

"I don't know," she said, "but it would've fit. Anyone having access to instant cleaning, instant meals, and instant travel but forbidding its use is a doofus."

"Agreed. Back to your question. Devon said he didn't think the information would help him solve the murder but it would add interesting details to the backstory."

Mom rolled her eyes. "Doofus."

"We've talked about my relationships — or lack thereof — with Ted and Todd," I said. "What's the deal with you and Cary? Are you his Sophia Loren?"

"No. I'm afraid I lack both the accent and the boobs to pull that off." She smiled. "I like Cary. He's nice, and we have a lot in common. How many straight men have you ever met who could tell you who Edith Head was?"

"Not many." Actually, I don't think I'd ever met anyone besides Mom and Cary who knew who Edith Head was, but I didn't want to sidetrack her.

"I'm not falling in love, if that's what you're asking," she said, "and neither is he. We enjoy each other's company. I'll probably see him on occasion when I'm in Oregon, and if he's ever in California, he'll likely look me up."

"That's it?" I asked.

"That's it. Cottages with white picket fences are for young people . . . like you. So don't let that dream pass you by."

"Like you did?"

Mom began to pick around in her salad again, and I knew it was to avoid looking at me. "I had that for a while . . . with your dad. When he died, I was devastated. And I was left with a little girl to care for on my own. You and my career were the only things I could think about then." She paused. "I guess it got to be a habit. I know you're grown now, and you don't really need me anymore . . . but I still need you."

I set my salad on the coffee table and went over to the sofa to give her a hug. "I'll always need you, Mom. Always." I felt guilty about venting to Ted earlier about the fear that Mom would move to Tallulah Falls. And I *did* need her. I just needed to learn to depend less on her and more on myself.

We finished our salads in companionable silence. As we were packing up the containers and forks, Ella Redmond came into the shop.

"Hi," she said breathlessly. "I had to park the car down the street, and so I ran here because I was afraid you'd be closing."

"Nope," I said with a smile. "Tonight's a class night, so we'll be here for a while yet."

"That's good. I ran out of blue perle floss for my needlepoint project." She handed me the label and a piece of blue floss. "Will this help you find the right color?"

I took the label. "All I need is the number. But hang on to that floss, so we can be sure it matches up." I took the label and went to the perle flosses.

Ella trailed behind me. "I suppose you're wondering why I was having a drink with that reporter yesterday evening."

I found the floss with the number Ella needed and turned to her with a smile. "That's entirely your own business." I quickly compared it to the thread she was holding. As expected, it was a perfect match. "How many skeins of this do you think you'll need?"

"Two should do it." She pressed her lips together. "He — Mr. Reed, that is — came to the library and asked for my help researching Louisa Ralston. He said you and he were trying to discover the truth about her death."

I handed her two skeins of blue floss. "*He*'s trying. I was open to helping him at first, but now I'm not so sure."

"Why not?" she asked.

"I think he's only trying to solve her murder so he can turn it into an article or a book or a movie," I said. "He doesn't want justice. He wants to make a profit by exploiting the poor woman's death."

"But can't you have both?" She lifted her shoulders. "I mean, you want justice, right?"

"Of course I do."

"And he wants to turn a profit. So long as you both get what you want, what difference does it make?" She smiled slightly. "I mean, two heads — or I guess three, counting me — are better than one . . . and more likely to discover the truth."

"Why are you so interested in the Ralston case?" I asked.

"One, I find history and its mysteries fascinating," she said. "And, two, I lost my mother a few years back. It was from illness rather than something sudden like Mrs. Ralston's death, but I understand the loss Mrs. Ralston's family must feel . . . how it would help them gain closure to know the truth."

"I see."

"I'm also eager to learn if my initial theory

pans out, and whether Ivy is, in fact, a person."

"If that's true, why would Mrs. Ralston come here to ask for my help?" I asked. "Wouldn't you go to the police if you were trying to find a missing person or a long-lost relative?"

"I would, yes. But perhaps Mrs. Ralston had a reason for coming here rather than going to the professionals. Maybe she'd sought help from the authorities before, and they'd either refused or been unable to help her." Ella moved toward the counter. "Maybe Mrs. Ralston was acquainted with the person who owned this shop before you, or perhaps she intended to check with all the merchants on this block. Maybe she even heard that you'd helped find Mr. Enright's killer and thought you might help her, too. Who knows? But Mr. Reed isn't so bad. A little overbearing, maybe, but I do believe he means well."

"You could be right." I rang up the floss and started to put it in a bag.

"Oh, there's no need for that," Ella said. "I'll just drop it into my purse. Greener that way, right?"

"Right." I smiled. "Have a good evening."

"Wow," Mom said, after Ella had left, "she certainly was trying to champion Mr. Reed's cause, wasn't she?"

"Yes, she was. Do you think she's right about him?" I joined Mom in the sit-and-stitch square. "Do you think I should give him another chance to help me discover who killed Mrs. Ralston?"

Mom shook her head. "You don't know or trust that guy, and with good reason. You *do* know and trust Ted Nash. Plus he's in a much better position to help you than Devon Reed could ever be."

I nodded. "Excellent point."

"Besides, if this reporter sells Mrs. Ralston's story to the tabloids or whatever he chooses to do with it, do you want to be a part of that?"

"No," I said, "I've never wanted to be a part of that."

"Well, if you work with him, you will be. You can't help but be, darling. Guilt by association, birds of a feather, yadda, yadda."

I smiled. "I get what you're saying. No matter what, people would think I was profiting from whatever smarmy deal Devon Reed might make."

"Precisely."

"What about Ella's belief that Ivy is a person?" I asked.

"She may have something there. Did Louisa and her granddaughter get along well? If not, perhaps Louisa was searching for another relative — one she preferred over Eleanor — to leave her fortune to." She shrugged. "When I get to be in my late eighties or nineties, you'd better be especially nice to me."

"I'm especially nice to you now," I said.

She grinned. "Yeah, but I have to work with what I've got. It'll be interesting to see if Cary's mother remembers anything when she sees the sampler."

"I agree. If their great-grandmother made the sampler, I imagine it hung in someone's house — their grandmother's, maybe — for years. Wouldn't you think?"

"Yeah, I would." Mom turned to look at the sampler. "It appears that someone treasured that sampler and took excellent care of it."

"Until, of course, someone ripped out the original verse and put in the quote about the ivy."

"But even that was done with care," Mom said.

"I hope Ms. Ellis remembers the original verse," I said, "and that she can tell us who changed it and why."

Mom grinned. "You're expecting a lot from the old gal, you know. She might not remember a thing."

"Remember what Cary said? He said she remembers what happened far in the past better than she can recall what she had for lunch. After tasting one of her cook's lunches, I can't imagine anyone forgetting those."

# Chapter Nineteen

Ted insisted on driving himself to the Ellis house. He said he needed to have his own transportation on hand in case he was called in by Chief Singh. I rode with him in his black Impala, and we followed Cary and Mom.

"This really does feel weird, doesn't it?" I asked. "Here I wanted to do something to thank you for all your help, and this is what I come up with."

Ted laughed. "It'll be fun. Besides, maybe we can gain some better insights into Louisa Ralston's life."

"I hope so. Do you know if the Tallulah County police have any other leads — besides me, of course?"

He shook his head. "I'm afraid not. And neither do I, for that matter. The woman apparently led an exemplary life. She was charitable, everyone seemed to like her, she provided for all her relatives in her will. . . ."

He shrugged. "There's no motive."

I sighed and rested my head against the back of the seat. "Maybe it's about me. Maybe ruining *me* is the motive, and Mrs. Ralston was simply the first victim to come along on the morning of the attack."

"But you didn't know Mrs. Ralston," Ted said. "If I planned to ruin you by making it appear you'd killed someone, I'd kill someone close to you and plant possible motives."

"Someone close to me," I murmured. "Like Jill, maybe?"

"Exactly like Jill. She'd be the perfect victim if somebody wanted to set you up. You work with her every day, and she stands right there at the register. You could have conceivably caught her with her hand in the till, and a person could kill her without having her death on his conscience because she's an inanimate object."

I faked a gasp. "You'd better never let Jill hear you talking like that."

"Something tells me that unlike a certain person I'll do the courtesy not to name, she wouldn't get all sassy and self-righteous if I did tell her," he said.

"Tell her she's an inanimate object or that she'd be the perfect murder victim? She'd get sassy about *that* if she could." I giggled.

"We really are actors in a screwball comedy, aren't we? We're following my mother and her boyfriend to his mother's house, and we're discussing why my mannequin would make the perfect murder victim."

He held up his index finger. "The perfect murder victim *if* someone was trying to frame you."

"Right. When what we really need to determine is whose perfect victim was Mrs. Ralston?" I shook my head. "There has to be a motive somewhere, Ted. Someone had to have it in for her personally."

"And don't forget Adam Gray," he said. "He was Mrs. Ralston's trusted adviser, and the same method was used. He had to have been killed for the same reason. We just have to figure out what it is."

"Is there any way you can poke around in Mr. Gray's office?"

"Out of my jurisdiction, remember? And Tallulah County is being fairly tight-lipped." He glanced at me. "But we'll figure it out, all right?"

"If you say so."

The drive to Ms. Ellis' house was a fairly quick one. We detoured only once, to pick up dinner, and Ted and I sat in the car parked beside Cary's Mercedes while he and Mom went into the Chinese restaurant to get the food.

Ms. Ellis had a beautiful home. It was easy to imagine Cary growing up here and becoming more and more enamored of the thought of being like Cary Grant. The large white house had a Spanish influence with arched windows and doorways and a red tile roof. The lawn was immaculate, and even though it was winter, I could see where flower beds had been primed for spring.

Mom, Ted, and I followed Cary inside. A tiny wisp of a woman with silver hair and blue eyes came to meet us in the foyer. She was wearing a high-necked tea-length aquamarine dress and a strand of pearls knotted at the bottom.

"Hello, my dears," she said. "Thank you for coming and for bringing dinner. Isabel has the night off, you know."

"I do know," Cary said. "Is Chinese all right, Mother?"

"Chinese will be wonderful," she said, with a smile. "I haven't had it since the last Friday evening you brought dinner."

Cary shrugged at Mom. "So, I'm predictable." He then introduced us all around.

I felt myself drawn to Ms. Ellis immediately. I could see the resemblance between her and her sister, but I felt that in their younger days, Ms. Ellis probably outshone even Louisa. She had an impish charm that made her eyes sparkle, and there was the perpetual hint of a smile around her mouth. I just hoped she would be able to tell me something that would help me figure out who had killed her sister.

"Come on into the dining room," she said. "I've got everything set up for us."

The table was made to seat eight, and Ms. Ellis had placed the plates, silverware, and glasses so that we were in the seats facing each other, with no one seated at the ends of the table.

"Cary, dear, would you pour the bubble tea?" she asked.

He laughed. "You knew I was bringing Chinese, then, eh?"

"Of course." Ms. Ellis winked at me. "Have you ever had bubble tea, Marcy?"

"No, I haven't. What is it?"

"It's a wonderful Asian tea made with tapioca pearls," she said. "I make my own."

Cary poured us all a cup of bubble tea, and Ms. Ellis watched us expectantly as we took our first sip. It was very sweet and quite good.

"Will you share the recipe?" I asked.

"Yes. Remind me to give it to you before you leave."

"I'm terribly sorry about your sister, Ms. Ellis," I said.

"Thank you," she said. "I'm sorry, too. We talked every day, and I miss her so much."

"I'm sure you do," I said, removing my napkin from my plate to allow Cary to spoon sweet and sour chicken onto it. I wanted to ask Ms. Ellis if she knew anyone who would want to harm her sister, but now didn't seem the appropriate time.

"You're looking well today, Mother," Cary said. "How are you feeling?"

"I'm fine. I have epilepsy," she explained to the rest of us. "He fusses over me as if I'm a five-year-old. Beverly, Cary tells me you're a costume designer." She grinned. "I gave Cary the name Carrington Grant because I fell head over heels for Cary Grant in *An Affair to Remember.* Not like I was in love with my husband, Richard; it was just a silly crush. Do you ever fall victim to those?"

Mom laughed. "Do I ever! Marcella had better be glad she was a girl. Otherwise, she'd have had a name as long as the *Orient Express.* Let's see, Robert Redford Paul Newman Gregory Harrison James Dean Michael Landon Singer, maybe?"

"That *is* as long as the *Orient Express,*" Cary said. "And rather than Marcy, we'd have called her Bobby Dean?"

"Bobby Dean Singer?" Ted asked. "Change the *y* to an *ie,* and that would still work."

I put up my hands. "No, thank you. Besides, I'm way too old for a name change."

"Who are you named after, Ted?" Ms. Ellis asked.

"I'm named after my father, Theodore Nash Sr."

She chuckled. "I was lucky to be the younger daughter. Louisa was named after Uncle Louis, who always smelled like fish and cigars. I was named Millicent — or Millie — after our great-grandmother. I never met the lady myself, but Mother told me Grandma Millie always smelled of sugar cookies and talcum powder." She nodded at me. "I'm looking forward to seeing that sampler you brought. Mother had it hanging in our kitchen for years."

After dinner, Cary took Mom and Ted on a tour of the house while I showed the framed sampler to Ms. Ellis. She looked at it lovingly, and I could see that it took her back to her childhood. A faint smile played around her lips as she ran her hand tenderly over the frame. Then she appeared to read the verse and her smile turned into a frown.

"Did you change the verse?" she asked.

"No. I think Louisa must have. Do you remember the original verse?"

"Of course. It was from Proverbs 31." She wrinkled her brow. "Verses 28 and 29, if I'm not mistaken. It was, 'Her children arise up, and call her blessed; her husband also, and he praiseth her. Many daughters have done virtuously, but thou excellest them all.' Grandma Millie made it for her mother."

"That's beautiful," I said. "Why would Louisa change that? Does it have anything to do with *ivy?* When your sister came into my shop that morning, she was asking me to help her find ivy. I wonder now if Ivy might be a person."

"Hmm . . . I don't recall anyone named Ivy," Ms. Ellis said. "But I'll dwell on it a bit and see if I can remember anything."

"Why don't you keep this?" I asked. "You can put it in your own kitchen. I could just frame a photo of it for the shop."

"No, thank you. I appreciate the thought, dear, truly I do. But I'm afraid it appears Louisa has ruined it because of her hatred of Edward."

"I . . . I b-beg your pardon?" I asked.

"The verse," she said. "Cary said Louisa had replaced the original verse, but he didn't tell me she'd replaced it with this drivel."

I was sitting beside her, and I looked at the verse to try to determine what had made it so offensive to Ms. Ellis.

> His friends were those of his own blood or those whom he had known the longest;
> his affections, like ivy, were the growth of time, they implied no aptness in the object.

That Louisa had taken out the verse her great-grandmother had so lovingly dedicated to her mother could be part of it. To replace a Bible verse with a quote from *The Strange Case of Dr. Jekyll and Mr. Hyde* could certainly factor in. But there was something more . . . something to do with Edward.

"I don't understand," I said. "Do you think this verse has something to do with Edward Larkin?"

"You know about him, then? He broke her heart, and I can understand her anger toward him. But I don't know why she'd ruin Grandma Millie's sampler over him."

I frowned. "How does this verse have anything to do with Edward Larkin?"

"The quote is from that Robert Louis Stevenson story about Edward Hyde," she said. "He was the horrible alter ego of Henry Jekyll. Apparently, Louisa felt that *her* Edward was a Jekyll and Hyde himself. And after he left her, she must've felt compelled to keep a constant reminder of Edward's villainy."

"You really think that's all there is to this verse?" I asked. "You don't think it has anything to do with ivy?"

"Ivy . . ." Ms. Ellis seemed to stare at a spot just behind me. "I don't . . . No, I don't think so." She snapped herself out of her reverie. "What were we saying?"

I bit my lip. Was there a more delicate way to put this than to just blurt it out? I couldn't think of one. And I knew Cary would be bringing Mom and Ted back momentarily. "Ms. Ellis, do you know anyone who would have wanted to hurt your sister?"

"No. Everybody liked Louisa," she said. "Well, everybody except that blasted Edward Larkin. I don't know why he had to go off and leave her after promising he would marry her. She was so heartbroken that she left us and worked in Seattle for two years." She shook her head. "It was a terrible business."

"What about Adam Gray?"

"Oh, yes, I know Adam. He's a nice man. I believe he'd have been a good match for Louisa had she ever paid him any mind." She smiled. "Sometimes we don't see what's right in front of us, do we?" She looked down at the sampler tenderly. "Thank you for bringing this. It holds a lot of memories."

"Are you sure you won't keep it?" I asked.

"Oh, no, Marcy. Not all the memories it dredges up are good ones. Here." As she handed the sampler back to me, I chipped a nail on the corner of the frame. "I'm sorry to be so clumsy. I've gone and broken your nail."

"It wasn't your fault, Ms. Ellis."

"There's a bathroom down that hallway — first door on your right," she said. "You'll find a nail file in the medicine cabinet."

"Thank you." I slid my chair back from the table and went down the hall to the bathroom. It was odd to go through someone else's medicine cabinet — I felt as if I was snooping — but I opened the door and spotted the nail file. I repaired my broken nail, and as I put the nail file back on the shelf, I accidentally knocked a medicine bottle to the floor. I picked it up to put it back where it belonged and noticed the label.

Halumet.

# Chapter Twenty

It was raining when Ted drove me home, and the rhythmic *swish-swoosh* sound of the windshield wipers was almost hypnotic. I'd told him about my inadvertent discovery of Halumet in Ms. Ellis' medicine cabinet, and we were discussing what it could mean.

"Had she been guilty of anything, she wouldn't have directed you to that medicine cabinet for a nail file," Ted said.

"I agree, but it does make me concerned about Cary." I sighed. "I wish Mom had agreed to come back with us."

"So do I, but you came at us all out of left field with that suggestion. 'Hey, I know! Why don't you ride back with us, Mom, so Cary can stay here a while longer with Ms. Ellis?' "

"I do not talk like that," I said.

"Agreed. But it was the best I could do." Ted tilted his chin. "If Cary lived with his mother, it might make more sense, but he has an apartment closer to his store, right?"

"You mean, for Mom to have ridden back with us or for him to be a suspect in Mrs. Ralston's death?" I asked.

"Both. As a police officer, I keep going back to motive. The man doesn't have one, as far as I can tell. Mrs. Ralston remembered him in her will and gave him a tidy sum of money. That's more than most nephews get."

"True," I said. "But who else had access to Ms. Ellis' house? And why was there Halumet in her medicine cabinet?"

"Ms. Ellis told us she had epilepsy. Certain central nervous system depressants are used to treat or prevent epileptic seizures, and I imagine Halumet is one of them," he said. "As for who has access to Ms. Ellis' medicine cabinet, it's hard to say. We know she has a cook. She probably has nursing assistants come in on a regular basis."

"So it gives us another lead?" I asked.

He smiled. "It gives us a terrific lead, and I'll be sure to pass my information along to Detectives Ray and Bailey."

He pulled into my driveway. Mom and Cary hadn't left when we did, but Mom had promised to be along soon. He cut off the engine and told me to sit tight. I thought he was merely being chivalrous until I noticed him looking all around the property as he made his way to my side of the car.

He opened the door and offered me his hand. I took it and said, "What a gentleman."

"Good breeding," he replied, continuing to look around the property.

Angus began barking from the backyard.

"Be there in a minute, Angus," I called.

Ted walked me to the front door. I took out my keys and unlocked the door. As I flipped on the lights and dropped my purse on the hall table, I noticed Ted's gaze taking in every aspect of the foyer and the living room.

"What?" I asked.

He looked down at me. "What?"

"You became my bodyguard the second you pulled into the driveway," I said. "Do you think I'm in danger?"

"I doubt it," he said, "but it's not a chance I'm willing to take. And you shouldn't, either." He placed his hands lightly at my waist. "Please be extra careful until this mess is resolved."

"I will."

I knew he wanted to kiss me and that he was waiting for me to give him a sign that I wanted him to. *Did* I want him to? I'd been trying to keep my distance from both him and Todd, but sometimes I realized how nice it would be to have a relationship again. I looked up at Ted, who stood well above a foot taller than me . . . his dark hair with the prematurely gray "highlights" . . . those blue eyes. One little kiss wouldn't really hurt, would it?

I stepped in closer. "Thank you."

His hands slid around my back and he bent forward to touch his lips to mine. I stood on my tiptoes to slide my hands up his muscular shoulders and around his neck as we kissed.

Angus' loud bark interrupted our embrace. I gave Ted a rueful grin. "I'd better let him in."

"Yeah. You'd better." He followed me through to the kitchen and gave the backyard the once-over as I opened the door for Angus.

"I should be going," Ted said as we returned to the living room. "Lock up after me, all right?"

"I always keep my doors locked, Detective."

He brushed my cheek with the back of his hand and left.

I turned on the fireplace, sat in my white suede club chair, and took out my phone to check my messages. There was one from

Devon and one from Todd. Devon's message was scolding me for having my calls go straight to voice mail when I knew he'd be calling about dinner that night. Todd was asking what time we were going to the auction.

I'd just retrieved the remote and flicked on the television when Mom came in. She gave Angus a pat, hung up her coat and scarf, and turned to me with a smile.

"Did he kiss you good night?" she asked.

I rolled my eyes, but I couldn't help the hint of a smile. "Yeah. Did Cary kiss you good night?"

"Yes, but I want to know about you. Did you enjoy your evening with Ted?"

"I did, but can we not get into this right now?" I nodded toward the sofa. "Come on and sit down and let's find a corny old movie to watch."

She sat on the sofa, kicked off her shoes, and stretched out her legs. "Why not get into it now? I see you have your cell phone out. Did Todd call while you were out with Ted?"

"Yes. He wants to know what time we're going to the auction tomorrow morning."

"Oh, yeah," she said. "I'd forgotten about that. What time *are* we going?"

"I thought we should be there when it

begins at nine. I open the shop at ten. I'm thinking maybe whoever killed Mrs. Ralston will be there."

"And that they'll want what?" Mom asked. "How will we identify this person or persons?"

"I don't know. I just have to do something. Maybe whoever the killer is — if he . . . or she . . . is at the auction — will behave suspiciously. So we — in particular, you — have to keep your eye on everyone there." I sighed. "I can only stay an hour unless I close the shop. And I hate to do that, because Saturday is generally one of my busiest days."

"I'll stay for the duration of the auction, and I'll watch out for murderous behavior. I've worked on enough mystery movie sets that I should know it when I see it," she said. "What piece were you interested in again? The umbrella stand?"

"Yes, and I'm guessing they'll auction off the smaller items first. I plan to bid on that if they sell it before I leave."

"I'll catch a ride back to the shop with Cary. Have you called and told Todd what time we're leaving?"

"Not yet. I will in a few minutes." I paused, uncertain of how to proceed. "You really like Cary, don't you?"

"Marcella, we've already had this discussion today. Must we have it again?"

"Listen, Mom, I'm glad you like him and that you're having fun. But I just . . . Well, I want you to be cautious. There was Halumet in his mother's medicine cabinet," I said. "I saw it when I went in there to get a nail file."

She cocked her head. "So?"

"So doesn't that kinda make Cary a suspect in Louisa Ralston's death?"

"Not in my book," she said. "Cary had no reason to kill his aunt, and neither did his mother — in case you're thinking she's the villain next."

"I'm not accusing anyone, Mom. I'm just asking you to be careful."

"Noted and appreciated. Thank you."

"Are you angry with me for bringing this up?" I asked.

"No, but I know Cary isn't a killer."

"What makes you so sure?"

She grinned. "Cary Grant never played a villain." She winked, picked up her shoes, and headed for the stairs. "I'm off to take a bath and let you return Todd's call." She looked back over her shoulder and made a funny face at me. "Vixen."

"I'm not a vixen," I said. "Unlike you, I don't have the upper hand. I just can't call up Ted and Todd and ask which of them has never played a villain or a heartbreaker before."

"Ah, yes," Mom said. "If only life were like a movie script."

"Mine is," I said. "Only it's currently being directed by Alfred Hitchcock."

She smiled. "I'd have loved to have worked with Hitchcock."

She went on upstairs, and I returned Todd's call.

"Hey, there," he said. "I'm just leaving the Brew Crew. I cut out early since I knew we'd have to be at the auction early tomorrow morning. Where've you been all evening?"

"Having dinner at Ms. Ellis' house. She's Cary's mother . . . and Mrs. Ralston's sister." I neglected to mention that Ted had come along.

"I'll bet that was interesting."

"More than you know," I said. "Can you be here at about eight thirty in the morning? The auction begins at nine, and I'd like to get a good spot."

"Sure, would you like me to bring breakfast?" he asked.

"No. If you can be here at eight, I'll make Mom cook."

Todd laughed. "Sounds like a plan. I'll see

you then."

A crowd had already gathered by the time Mom, Todd, and I arrived at the Ralston home. Sadie drove up as we were getting out of the Jeep.

"Wonder if they'll have anything I can afford," she said as we walked toward the house. "I'd love to get an antique coffeepot or teapot for the shop."

Cary had been watching for us, and he hurried over as soon as he saw us approaching.

"Good morning, ladies . . . Ted," he said.

Gulp.

"Todd," Todd replied, correcting him.

"Of course. My mistake." Cary took Mom's arm. "I've been saving you a spot over here near the porch." He handed the four of us auction paddles.

"Don't you need one?" Mom asked. "Aren't you planning to bid on anything?"

"No," Cary said. "I'm here out of morbid curiosity more than anything else." He spotted someone above the crowd and waved her over. "It's Eleanor."

Eleanor wove through the crowd. "I never dreamed there would be so many people here. I hope they're bidders and not merely gawkers."

Mom laughed. "Nothing worse than a window-shopper at an auction, right?"

"That's right," Eleanor said. "Then what would I do with all this stuff? Sell it online?"

The auctioneer came out onto the porch and stood in front of a podium. He rapped his gavel and called for silence as he announced the first item. It was the umbrella stand Mr. Gray had told me about.

"I put that at the top of the list," Cary whispered to me. "I know it's what you're here for."

"Thank you," I said with a smile. Mom was right. He could never be a villain.

"The first item," said the auctioneer, "is a nineteenth-century cast-iron umbrella stand from Chase Brothers and Company of Boston. This piece retails for approximately three thousand five hundred dollars, but the starting bid today is a hundred dollars. Do I hear a hundred?" Exactly what I had been looking for. It was absolutely gorgeous. Sometimes a girl needs to splurge.

I raised my paddle.

"That is beautiful," Sadie whispered. "And it retails for three thousand five hundred dollars? Whoa."

"I have a hundred dollars. Do I hear a hundred and fifty dollars? I have a hundred and fifty. Do I hear a hundred seventy-five dollars?"

I raised my paddle again.

The auctioneer continued. "I have a hundred seventy-five; do I hear two hundred? I have two hundred from the man in the black jacket. Do I have two hundred twenty-five?"

I raised my paddle, looking around to see who was bidding against me. Height was not on my side. "Who's bidding against me?" I whispered to Todd.

"I have two hundred twenty-five from the lady in the red trench coat," the auctioneer said. "Do I have two hundred fifty? I have two hundred fifty. Thank you, sir."

"It's Devon Reed," Todd said softly.

I ground my teeth and raised the paddle when the auctioneer asked for a bid of $275. "I'm not going over three hundred dollars," I said.

"Nonsense," Mom said. "We can't let *him* win it."

"Absolutely not," Sadie said.

"I know he's only bidding on it to spite me," I said.

"Which is exactly why I refuse to let him win it," Mom said.

"I have two hundred seventy-five," the auctioneer said.

"I bid one thousand dollars." I recognized the voice as that of Devon Reed.

"If he wants it that badly," I said, "he can have the stupid thing." I had to hold Mom's arm at her side to keep her from bidding $1,025.

"Going once, going twice, and sold to the man in the black jacket."

"I'm sorry, Marcy," Cary said. "It's the only umbrella stand Aunt Louisa had."

"That's all right, Cary. I'll find one somewhere," I said. "Besides, we're mainly here to support Eleanor."

Eleanor turned to me and smiled. "Thank you, Marcy. I do appreciate that."

"Right you are, Marcy," Cary said. "Thank you for reminding me of the real reason we're here . . . to support one who has been a support to us over the years." He patted Eleanor's shoulder.

"I appreciate that, Cary. How's your mom, by the way?" she asked.

"She's wonderful," he said. "We visited her just last night." He turned to Mom. "Eleanor used to be a nurse. Everyone in the family used to hound her for medical advice, and she helped with Mother from time to time."

"You're not a nurse anymore, then?" Mom asked.

"No. It's a trying profession," Eleanor said. "It proved to be more than I could take."

"What do you do now?" I asked.

"I'm going back to school to get a paralegal degree," she said.

"Good for you," Todd said. "It's great you were able to start over in another career rather than having to stick with one you disliked."

"I agree wholeheartedly," I said, although somehow I couldn't quite picture the rough-around-the-edges Eleanor as ever having been a good nurse.

# CHAPTER TWENTY-ONE

Todd and I left the auction soon after Devon Reed bought the umbrella stand. Mom and Sadie stayed behind, and I was eager to see if either of them learned anything or brought anything home later.

I dropped Todd off at the Brew Crew, and I went on to work. I thought about going back home to get Angus, but Mom and I would be there with him tonight. Plus, it was partly sunny today, and he would likely enjoy romping in the backyard.

I'd got in a shipment of pattern books. I put most of them on display, but took one of each to the sit-and-stitch square to thumb through them. I love looking at new patterns. The problem is I want to stitch them all.

Vera Langhorne stopped in to see if I had any Victorian pillowcase designs I thought she could do. "I bought the bedroom suite, Marcy! I have a moving crew bringing it later this afternoon."

I smiled. "I'm so happy for you."

"So am I. Those pieces are going to look gorgeous in my bedroom. Now I need some linens to make the room even prettier."

I showed her some pieces that she could embroider using redwork or blackwork.

She frowned. "I'm not very familiar with either of those."

"They're easy to do," I said.

She bit her lip. "Maybe I'll see what I can find in some linen boutiques tomorrow before I jump headlong into embroidering pillowcases." She started to leave. "By the way, did you get the umbrella stand you wanted?"

"Afraid not," I said. "I was outbid."

"I'll see what I can find while I'm out shopping tomorrow," Vera said on her way out.

I shook my head and sat back down to continue going through the pattern books. Thinking about Devon Reed, however, made me think of Ella Redmond. I decided to give her a quick call at the library. Her phone went directly to voice mail.

"Hi, Ella. It's Marcy Singer. I just wanted to tell you I think the theory that Ivy was a person Louisa Ralston knew is unlikely. Cary's mother, Ms. Ellis, didn't recall anyone named Ivy and thought Louisa had changed the verse to remind herself that Edward Larkin was a jerk. Talk with you later."

I finished looking at the pattern books, but rather than putting them on display, I fanned the ones I'd been perusing onto the coffee table. That way customers coming in to sit and stitch could look at them and either get ideas or decide to purchase books of their own.

Business picked up after Vera dropped in, and I thought maybe the auction crowd was dispersing and starting to wend its way into town to shop. I sold needlepoint canvas, skeins of yarn, cross-stitch cloth, and both cotton and metallic embroidery floss.

When the bells over the door jingled around eleven a.m., I raised my head and smiled. The smile faded as Devon Reed strolled into the shop.

"Hi, Marcy. Sorry about buying the umbrella stand out from under you, but it'll look nice by the coatrack in my apartment."

"I'm glad you're putting it to good use," I said stiffly.

"I still think we could've worked well together, but you've made it clear you're not interested in learning the truth about Mrs. Ralston." He pursed his lips. "Besides,

Ella and I are doing a fine job of putting all the pieces of this puzzle together."

"Good," I said. "I hope it works out for you."

As I was talking, the door opened and Ella Redmond came in. "Speak of the devil," I said to Devon.

"Is that why my ears are burning?" Ella asked with a slight smile. "Actually, I'm glad you're here, Devon. I wanted to ask you if you'd accompany me to dinner in Lincoln City this evening. I have a lead I think you'll be particularly interested in."

"I'd love to," Devon said, looking at me and arching a brow. "Marcy, would you like to join us?"

"I'm sorry, but I can't. Mom and I need to go by the funeral home and pay our respects to Mr. Gray's family."

"I got your message," Ella said, "but I have to disagree with you, Marcy. I still think Ivy was a person. In fact, I think she might've been Louisa's daughter."

I shook my head. "Louisa had only one child, and it was a boy."

"By Frank Ralston," Ella said. "What about Edward Larkin? I believe that's why Louisa was *working* at the orphanage after Edward joined the army." She looked at Devon. "I'm on my lunch break and need to get back to the library. Call me later, and we'll work out the details on dinner." She smiled at me. "I'll see you Tuesday evening."

"If you change your mind about dinner," Devon said, "I'm sure Ella wouldn't mind your tagging along. We could always use your input."

"Thank you, but somehow I think she would mind."

"Jealous?" he asked.

"Not at all. Have a terrific time."

He winked and then turned and left. I felt like throwing a pencil at the back of his arrogant, obnoxious head.

I was sitting at the counter ruminating over the possibility of Louisa Ralston's having had Edward Larkin's child when Mom came in.

"Whoa," she said. "You look like you're a million miles away."

"More like a million years," I said. I explained about Devon's and Ella's almost simultaneous visits to the shop and Ella's belief that Louisa Ralston had been working at the orphanage because she had been pregnant with Edward Larkin's baby. "What do you think?"

She sat on the red chair, took off her shoes, and put her feet on the ottoman. "It's possible. And it was such a social taboo back then that even if the family knew, they wouldn't have dared speak of it."

"So you think Louisa Ralston could've had a baby without her family even knowing about it?" I asked.

"Maybe. Unwed mothers were terribly ostracized then and usually forced to give up their babies for adoption whether they wanted to or not."

"That's sad."

"It is," she agreed. "It reminds me of the Barbara Stanwyck movie *No Man of Her Own.* Pregnant Barbara has been dumped by her rotten, no-good boyfriend, and she has nowhere to go. She's on a train, and the train crashes, killing a newly married couple. Barbara assumes the married woman's identity — the parents had never met her — and goes to live with the woman's in-laws. I think she winds up marrying the husband's brother by the end of the movie."

I nodded slowly. "So you think Louisa went to the Ralston home posing as a pregnant widow?"

"No, Miss Sassy, I'm only saying that was a good movie and that it's entirely possible Louisa found herself with child and with nowhere to go. So she went to work in the orphanage until her broken heart was mended. Which is code for 'until the baby was born and adopted.' "

"Then that baby *could* be Ivy," I said. "That could be who Mrs. Ralston was looking for."

"Too bad Adam Gray is dead. That sounds like something he should've known."

"Shoulda, coulda, woulda, but maybe not," I said. "He never said anything about it to me, and — especially with Louisa dead — why wouldn't he?" I shrugged. "Maybe his secretary will know something."

"Couldn't hurt to ask."

Mom wore her dove gray suit to Mr. Gray's visitation, and I wore a black suit.

"I'm glad I brought something suitable for a funeral," she said. "Although, to be honest, I never dreamed I'd *need* something to wear to a funeral while I was here . . . much less *two* funerals."

"I know." I sighed. "Welcome to my world."

"I'm not so sure I like your world. Please consider coming back home to California."

I told her I'd think about it, and we went inside. Riley was there, looking lovely in a navy maternity dress.

"Hi, guys," she said when we approached. "How're you doing?"

"Fine," I said. "You look terrific."

She smiled. "For a blimp, you mean?"

"For anyone," Mom said.

"By the way," I said, "do you have all the ladies in town knitting and crocheting blankets?"

"Not all of them," she said. "There are a few knitters and crocheters I've commissioned to do blankets and layette sets. Are you mad that I didn't ask you?"

"Oh, no," I said. "I just wondered why there has been a run on white yarn in the shop. So, thank you for that."

"You're quite welcome. I figured I'd given you enough to do. . . . Not that you're finished yet."

"I'm so sorry about Mr. Gray," I said.

"Yeah, me, too. Did you bring your magnifying glass so you could look for clues?" she teased.

"No. At least, I'm not being that conspicuous." I nodded toward Mr. Gray's secretary. "What do you know about her?"

"Marsha? She's got the personality of a mop, but she knows her stuff," Riley said. "Or I guess I should say she knows Mr. Gray's stuff. She's been his only secretary for the past twenty or so years."

"Wonder if she'd know anything about Mrs. Ralston's past," I said.

Riley closed one eye and wrinkled her

nose. "Maybe. Maybe not. Mr. Gray was protective of Louisa. If she had secrets she wanted kept, he'd have kept them even from Marsha." She gave a slight shrug. "Still, now that he's gone, he'd have wanted to fulfill not only his own last wishes but those of his clients, too . . . especially Mrs. Ralston. It wouldn't hurt to talk with Marsha. Want me to go with?"

"Please," I said. "She doesn't strike me as very friendly."

"You two go ahead," Mom said. "I see Cary, and I want to say hello."

Riley and I walked over to Marsha. She was wearing a brown tweed suit and brown shoes, and she was crumpling a tissue in her hand.

Riley hugged Marsha. "I'm truly sorry about Adam. Dad, Mom, and I loved him very much. Mom would've been here, but she has a terrible cold."

"Thank you," Marsha said. "And thank her for the flowers. They're lovely. They'd have meant a lot to him."

"You've met Marcy, haven't you?" Riley asked.

Marsha nodded stiffly. "You were there that morning."

"Yes, I was," I said. "I, too, am really sorry for your loss. Mr. Gray seemed like a delightful person."

"He was."

"Was anyone besides me there that morning?" I asked. "I understand Mr. Gray's appointment canceled, but was I the only one who came to see him?"

She shook her head. "No, Mr. Ellis came by . . . and Eleanor. Eleanor had been coming by on a regular basis. She's studying to be a paralegal, you know. Mr. Gray was letting her gain experience in his office."

"Anyone else?" Riley asked.

"No," Marsha said. "What's this about?"

"We were simply wondering about Mrs. Ralston's charity," Riley said. "What will happen to it now that Mr. Gray is gone?"

"If unclaimed within three months, the funds will go to a children's home in Portland," Marsha said.

"Unclaimed?" I asked. "By whom?"

Marsha's eyes darted from side to side. "Excuse me. I need to speak with Judge Hoenbeck."

Riley turned her mouth down at the corners as Marsha made her hasty exit. "We need to dig a little deeper there."

# Chapter Twenty-Two

On Sunday afternoon, Mom and I were in the living room watching the movie she'd told me about yesterday — *No Man of Her Own.* She'd gotten me interested in it, and I'd had to rent it. The credits were rolling, and Mom and I were dabbing our eyes and wiping our noses with tissues from the box I'd put on the coffee table in anticipation of our reaction to the movie.

When the phone rang, Mom turned off the TV and said she'd take Angus for a walk. It was Riley on the phone.

"Hi," she said. "Keith went to play basketball with some friends, so I got on the laptop to research that charity Marsha told us about."

"What were you able to dig up?" I asked.

"Louisa Ralston set up a trust about twenty years ago under the name Ivy League. That seemed weird to me, so I did a search through the corporation commission for nonprofits or sole proprietorships under the name Ivy League."

"Ivy League," I said. "Like the schools?"

"Yes, although I'm sure she only used that as a cover. Maybe it was so she could tell her husband she was instituting a girls' scholarship fund at an Ivy League school or something."

"Then Frank's name isn't on the trust?" I asked.

"No. It's in Louisa's name and Ivy League only," Riley said. "The trust was to revert to Ivy League through its administrator, Adam Gray, upon Louisa's death."

"So what happens now that Adam is dead?"

"The same rules apply," said Riley, "only now the trust will have to be administered by someone else. Here's the catch. If Ivy League doesn't claim the trust within three months of Louisa's death, the money in that trust reverts to Sunshine Manor, which seems to be some sort of children's home in Portland."

"Seems to be?"

"Yeah. I couldn't find any business records from Sunshine Manor, and I went back ten years."

"Do you think Sunshine Manor is now defunct?" I asked. "And if so, what happens to the trust in that case?"

"That's one of the things that's so strange about this whole deal," Riley said. "The clause stipulating that the money would revert to Sunshine Manor if unclaimed was added only about a year ago."

"But you couldn't find any tax records for them doing business?" I asked.

"Exactly."

"Which means what?"

"I think it means somebody was setting Louisa Ralston up in order to inherit the money that she'd earmarked for someone else," Riley said. "I believe Sunshine Manor is a dummy corporation."

"But wouldn't either Louisa or Adam Gray have checked that out before making the company a beneficiary of Louisa's will?"

"Of course," Riley said, "which is what makes me think the corporation was submitted to them by someone they both trusted."

"Were you able to find out anything else about Sunshine Manor?"

"Not yet," she said, "but I'm still digging. I did find out that Louisa Ralston set up a sole proprietorship with herself and — are you ready for this? — Ivy Larkin as the sole shareholders. She called the corporation Ivy League."

I gasped. "That means Louisa did have a

child by Edward Larkin."

"Right. But where is she?"

"We have to find out," I said.

"And we have to find out who's behind Sunshine Manor," Riley said.

When Mom and Angus returned, I told her what Riley had discovered. "I need to call Ella Redmond and tell her she was right about Ivy all along."

Mom started shaking her head. "Don't you dare."

"Why not?"

"All along you've said you don't want to help Devon Reed publish a bunch of garbage about Louisa Ralston," she said. "If you call Ella Redmond, you might as well make it a three-way call so he can hear it firsthand."

"I hadn't thought about that, but you're right. She made it obvious today that they're a team." I frowned. "How else can I track down Ivy Larkin?"

"I'll help you. Plus, Riley is working on it." Mom nodded. "If she can be found, we'll find her. Is the Tallulah County Historical Society open today?"

"I believe so," I said.

"That might be a good starting point."

We checked and learned the society was open until five o'clock. We had two hours.

Mom put Angus in the backyard, and I made a quick call to Riley to let her know what Mom and I were doing. She told us to keep her posted and said that she would continue searching online for information about Sunshine Manor.

When we arrived, no one but the desk clerk was around. Glad for some privacy, Mom and I took a brochure with a list of exhibits and their whereabouts.

"I'm going to start with some photographs," I said. "Maybe if I see a young Louisa Ralston, I'll recognize her."

"I'll look for records about the orphanage," Mom said.

The desk clerk was an elderly woman with tightly curled white hair. "May I help you with something?" she asked.

"Yes," I said. "We're looking for records pertaining to an orphanage or children's home that was located near here in the late nineteen thirties and early nineteen forties."

The woman nodded. "The Tipton-Haney Home. It was an orphanage, but the place had *volunteers* who were unwed mothers."

"Do you remember anything about the Tipton-Haney Home personally?" Mom asked. "Do you recall any of the volunteers who may have worked there?"

"Not really," the woman said. "They were

discreet." She smiled. "But, then, I was a little girl during its heyday, and I used to eavesdrop on my mother's quilting circle to hear the gossip."

"Did you ever hear any gossip about Louisa Ralston?" I asked.

"I did . . . although at the time, she was Louisa Connor. I remember her story because Louisa was a nice girl, came from a good family, and was as pretty as could be. I'd admired her and had hoped to grow up to be like her." The woman shook her head ruefully. "I know Louisa thought Edward Larkin was going to marry her."

"What was he like?" Mom asked.

"Oh, he was a rake," the woman said. "He was handsome, had dimples you could swim in, and eyes as blue as the sky. There wasn't a girl in Tallulah County who didn't have a crush on Edward. And he knew it."

Now was the time to ask a leading question. "How do you think Louisa got so taken in by him that she allowed herself to get pregnant with his baby?" I asked.

"She thought he was going to marry her, of course. Their engagement was in the newspaper and everything." The woman clicked her tongue as she shook her head ruefully.

"Then what happened?" I asked. "I heard

Edward enlisted in the army. Was he drafted?"

"No, I don't think so," she said.

"Then why didn't he and Louisa get married?" I asked. "You see, Louisa was in my shop the morning that she died, and she was asking me to help her find 'ivy.' I'm wondering now if Ivy might've been her daughter."

She shrugged. "It's possible. Even though Edward had the reputation of a skirt-chaser, he'd settled down and seemed committed to Louisa. No one imagined that he would jilt the poor girl so close to the wedding like he did. Men just didn't take their commitments that lightly back then."

Mom nodded. "And Louisa volunteered at Tipton-Haney House in order to have her child. Do you think she intended to keep the baby?"

"I don't know. When Louisa Connor volunteered at Tipton-Haney House, people were merely speculating," the woman said. "Had she left with a child, everyone would have known for certain she'd had the baby out of wedlock."

"But Louisa missed that baby," I said. "I think she was grieving for the child in her final days."

"I suspect you're right," the woman said.

"Why couldn't she have moved away?" I asked. "Or had someone else take the baby so she could still be a part of its life?"

The woman smiled. "My dear, those are questions only Louisa Ralston could have answered." She moved from around the counter and took us to a section of the museum dedicated to the Tipton-Haney House. "Let me know if I can be of further assistance to you." She looked at her watch. "We close in an hour."

We looked through the documents and photos pertaining to Tipton-Haney House. There was a framed group photo with an accompanying newspaper article that caught my eye.

"Mom, look." I pointed out the girl I thought to be Louisa and the baby from the locket. "These are the same photos from the locket. Louisa must've used the ones from this original photo."

"It does look like them," Mom agreed, "but why isn't Louisa holding her baby?"

Neither Louisa nor any of the younger girls in the photograph were holding babies. Some were standing with older children, holding the toddlers' hands or with their hands on the children's shoulders. All the babies, however, were held by elderly women.

The article explained that Tipton-Haney House employed social workers and accommodated young ladies who wished to learn to care for children. The article claimed that by living at Tipton-Haney House, the volunteers learned to run a household and meet the needs of a family.

"She isn't holding her baby," I said, "because Tipton-Haney House tried to debunk the idea that it was a home for unwed mothers. I think the Tipton-Haney House staff members and whoever these old ladies were — volunteers maybe — were really trying to protect these young women's reputations and do what they thought was best for them."

"Look," Mom said, pointing to some adoption records contained in a glass case. "They called the children by their first names only . . . to further protect the birth mothers, I suppose. See? Baby Anne . . . Baby Benjamin . . . Baby Lenore . . ."

"Baby Ivy," I said. "There it is." I looked closer. "Baby Ivy was adopted by Arthur and Mildred Sutherland."

As we started to leave the Tallulah County Historical Society, I asked the museum volunteer about Frank Ralston. "What was he like?" I asked. "Did he know people had questioned Louisa's reason for working at

Tipton-Haney House?"

"Frank Ralston was a vile-tempered man prone to drink," she said. "As I've already told you, Louisa was a lovely girl. And she came from a good family. When Frank Ralston started courting her, she couldn't very well turn him away."

"She married him to save her reputation?" I asked.

"I think so," the woman said.

"Do you believe she grew to love him?" I asked.

She smiled. "No one can truly speak about another's heart. I'd like to think she did. And they had that beautiful son."

"I'm sure she loved him," Mom said. "I heard he died."

"He did. He had an aneurysm. It was very sudden and very sad," the woman said. "Frank died not long after that of heart failure."

I had the sudden macabre thought that it might possibly have been heart failure by Halumet, although I seriously doubted the drug had even been developed at that time. I also doubted I would ever get to the point where I wouldn't question another death deemed heart failure.

"We should be going," I said. "It's almost time for you to close up. Thank you so much for your hospitality."

"Anytime," she said.

As Mom and I went out to get into the Jeep, I murmured, "Arthur and Mildred Sutherland. At least it's a start."

# CHAPTER TWENTY-THREE

When we got home, Mom started making dinner. I fed Angus and then called Riley to give her an update.

"I'm still searching for corporation information on Sunshine Manor," Riley said, "but I haven't found anything yet. I'll keep looking. In the meantime, you start feeding Arthur and Mildred Sutherland through genealogy sites."

"I will. I'll let you know if I find anything."

"Ditto."

"By the way," I said, "is Marsha still working in Mr. Gray's office?"

"She'll be there this coming week sorting through files, calling clients, and trying to get everything in order. Why?"

"I'm thinking of paying her a visit to see what — if anything — she knows about Ivy Larkin," I said.

When I hung up, I went to see if Mom needed any help in the kitchen. She had her sleeves rolled up and was making meatballs. I washed my hands and began helping her form the meat and put it in the frying pan.

"Did Riley have anything new?" she asked.

"Not yet. She told me to run the Sutherlands through some genealogy Web sites to see what I can come up with."

"I can do that while you're at work in the morning." She smiled. "You know I enjoy my lazy mornings. Besides, I have a videoconference with Tony Hammonds, the producer for the new movie, tomorrow morning."

"Have you worked with Mr. Hammonds before?" I asked.

"Once. He produced *Murderous Symphony.* He's a good guy . . . very easy to work for."

"Good. When do you have to get back?"

"Not for a week or so," she said. "I'm here for as long as you need me, sweetheart."

"I appreciate that, Mom, but don't let me get you in trouble or cost you a job. I'd never forgive myself."

"I've tossed the salad," she said, effectively changing the subject. "And we've almost got the meatballs formed. I've got the water boiling for the spaghetti. But what're we having for dessert?"

I rolled my eyes. "You could've just said

you didn't want to talk about it."

"No, seriously, what's for dessert? We need to live it up while I'm here."

Smiling, I opened the freezer, where I had a small strawberry cheesecake. "Will this do?"

"Perfectly."

I set the cheesecake on the counter to thaw. I really did hope this matter with Louisa Ralston would be resolved before Mom left to go back to work.

I set the alarm and got up early Monday morning. I wanted to go by MacKenzies' Mochas and get coffee and muffins to take to Adam Gray's office. If I got there just after Marsha did, I would have at least an hour to talk with her before I needed to get back and open the Seven-Year Stitch.

I filled Angus' bowl with food, and as I got dressed, I let him play in the backyard. I brought him back in before I left. He whimpered, but I kissed him on top of the head and assured him he'd have company as soon as Mom woke up.

It was a good thing the coffee shop itself was warm when I arrived at MacKenzies' Mochas, because my reception there was decidedly cool. Sadie was behind the counter this morning.

"Hey, there," I said, sitting on a stool. "Did you wind up buying anything at the auction?"

"No."

I frowned but wasn't ready to give up yet. I wasn't sure if I'd done something or if she was upset about something else. "Well, did you have a good weekend?"

She shrugged. "I guess so. Probably not as good as you had . . . with your *two* dates."

"I don't know that I'd call either of them dates."

"No, I suppose not. Todd was more of a standby in case you needed some muscle to help you carry home something from the auction." She went to help another customer.

So Sadie had found out about my date with Ted, and she wasn't happy about it. Part of me wanted to stay and explain, but part of me — the biggest part — simply did not want to deal with an attitude this early on a Monday morning. I got up and left, thinking there had to be another coffee shop between here and Adam Gray's office.

There was. After all, this is the Pacific Coast we're talking about. Coffeehouses are as plentiful as gas stations . . . maybe more so.

I bought two cappuccinos and a box of

assorted muffins, and everything was still piping hot when I arrived at Adam Gray's office. I walked in but did not see Marsha.

"Marsha?" I called.

"Who's there?"

"It's Marcy Singer. I've brought cappuccino and muffins."

"I'm in Adam's office. Come on back."

I found Marsha wearing jeans, a faded sweatshirt, and hiking boots. Her face was devoid of makeup, and her copper hair had been pulled back.

"Housecleaning?" I asked.

She nodded. "Let me wash my hands, and I'll be right back."

She stepped out of the office, and I placed the cappuccinos and muffins on the desk. I glanced around to see what Adam might have been working on the morning he died, but the desk was too messy to really tell. Marsha returned and sat in Adam's chair. I sat in one of the chairs in front of the desk.

"What kind of muffins did you bring?" she asked, licking her lips as she peered into the box.

"I didn't know what kind you might like, so there's a banana nut, a blueberry, an apple cinnamon, and a chocolate chip."

"Which one do you want?"

"You pick first," I said, sipping my cappuccino.

She chose the chocolate chip, and I settled on the blueberry.

"Thank you," she said. "This is awfully nice of you." She tore off a piece of her muffin. "But why do I feel you have an ulterior motive?"

"Maybe I do. I'd like to know who killed your boss . . . but I think you want to know that, too."

She popped the bite of muffin into her mouth and chewed thoughtfully. "I do . . . but I don't want to be next."

"Do you think Mr. Gray's death had anything to do with Louisa Ralston?" I asked.

"Possibly." She was still being vague. I could see her reasoning, but I didn't have time to tap-dance around her fears.

"Let me lay out a scenario for you," I said, "and you tell me whether I'm hot or cold."

She simply stared at me and tore off another bite of her muffin.

"Ever since Frank Ralston died however many years ago," I continued, "Louisa has been looking for the child she had when she was a teenager and had to put up for adoption at the Tipton-Haney House."

Marsha's jaw dropped. "Louisa had a child when she was a teenager?"

"So you didn't know?"

"No," she said. "Are you sure?"

"My mother, Riley, and I were able to piece together much of Louisa's story yesterday," I said. "We think Louisa had a daughter by Edward Larkin and that she has been looking for her daughter, Ivy. I think she wanted Ivy to have the majority of her vast estate . . . sort of to make it up to Ivy for having to abandon her all those years ago. And I was sure Adam would have been helping her with her search."

"I don't think he was. If he had been, I'd have known about it."

"I believe Louisa was afraid she might have been unable to find her daughter, so she had Adam set up a trust for a corporation called Ivy League, in which Louisa and Ivy Larkin were the sole proprietors. But if Louisa died and Ivy couldn't be found, the money would go to a children's home called Sunshine Manor."

"You're right about that," Marsha said. "Adam did set up a trust for Louisa in both her name and the name Ivy Larkin."

"But you're telling me Adam didn't know Ivy was Louisa's daughter?" I asked.

"He might've suspected, but I don't think he ever knew for certain. He put Louisa Ralston on a pedestal. He would never have admitted anything — even to himself — that might have knocked her off it." She pinched off another piece of her muffin. "But you seem to know all about the trust, so why do you need me?"

"To find out why Adam was killed," I said. "And Louisa, too, for that matter." I took another sip of cappuccino and leaned forward. "Riley was able to figure out that Sunshine Manor is not a children's home but a dummy corporation. I think Adam found that out, too."

Marsha shook her head. "I don't think so. Although he had begun trying to find one of the nonprofit's principals after Louisa died so he could discuss the trust with them."

"Was he also attempting to find Ivy Larkin?" I asked. "I saw something at the historical society that said Ivy was adopted by a Mildred and Arthur Sutherland," I said.

"He was trying to find Ivy Larkin in order to disburse the trust, but he didn't really believe anyone would ever find her. He had Eleanor looking into it, but that was mainly in order to give her practice in doing record searches."

"Did Eleanor find anything?"

"Only that a child named Ivy Larkin was adopted by the Sutherlands, as you already know. She also learned that the Sutherlands had left the state of Oregon and relocated in Kansas or somewhere. I typed up her notes to give to Adam." Marsha took a sip of her cappuccino and kept the warm cup in her hands.

"What about Edward Larkin?" I asked. "Did Louisa ever hear anything more from him? Or did he ever look for the baby?"

"I have no idea."

I frowned. "How did Mrs. Ralston get mixed up with Sunshine Manor?"

"She was looking for a children's home to donate the money to if she was unsuccessful in her attempts to find Ivy. She didn't want to give it to some large organization. She wanted to keep it local . . . give the money to a smaller children's organization here in Oregon."

"That's nice," I said.

"Mrs. Ralston was top-notch," said Marsha. "Anyway, her sister had told her about Sunshine Manor and given her a brochure. Sunshine Manor was located in Portland, was a large home for needy and abandoned children, and was run by a Christian foundation. Mrs. Ralston thought it would be perfect."

"Do you still have the brochure?" I asked.

"I think so. It's here in Mrs. Ralston's

file." She got up, opened a file cabinet and flipped through the files until she located Mrs. Ralston's. She took out the brochure and handed it to me.

When I saw the cream-colored Victorian mansion with the spire on the left towering above the gazebo, my jaw dropped.

"What is it?" Marsha asked.

"This isn't Sunshine Manor," I said. "It's the Victorian Mansion at Los Alamos. It's a bed-and-breakfast." I recognized it because Mom and I had stayed there one weekend.

"So Sunshine Manor really was a dummy corporation. No wonder Adam couldn't locate any of the administrators."

I looked through the brochure and saw photographs of children and happy administrators. Whoever had made this brochure had "borrowed" their location from Los Alamos, so I figured the photos had been borrowed as well.

"May I make a copy of this?" I asked Marsha.

"Keep it. Just let me have it back when you're through. I don't know who's going to handle the administration of Mrs. Ralston's estate now that Adam's gone" — she shook her head — "but I don't think the new administrator will need that garbage, do you?"

"No," I said. "But I might be able to use it to track down the person who set Mrs. Ralston up."

# Chapter Twenty-Four

I stopped by the house on my way to work to pick up Mom and Angus. I ran inside and called to Mom because I really needed to grab them and get to the shop.

"Hi, darling," Mom called from the top of the stairs. "You and Angus go on to the shop. I need to stay here and pack."

"You're leaving?"

"Yeah. After the producer and I talked, we realized we need to meet in person and collaborate on sketches, materials we plan to use, and things like that," she said. "Trying to pin it all down electronically just won't work with what we're doing."

"Maybe I should go with you," I said.

Mom started down the stairs. "Why? Did something happen?"

"Sort of. Do you remember the Victorian Mansion at Los Alamos? The cast and crew of *Summer Showers* had a party on the set, and you were too tired to drive us all the way back home."

"That's right," she said. "So we stopped there and stayed in the Egyptian Room. Lucky for us it was available. As I recall, it's the only room with a balcony."

"Right." I took the brochure for Sunshine Manor out of my pocket. "Check this out."

She came down the steps to look at the brochure. "This says Sunshine Manor, but it's the back entrance to the Victorian Mansion at Los Alamos."

"I know. I want to go there and check their books from one to two years ago to see who might've been there and used this photograph to set Louisa Ralston up for this scam."

Mom opened the brochure and frowned as she perused its contents. "You don't think this could actually be Sunshine Manor, do you? Maybe it only *looks* remarkably like the Victorian Mansion at Los Alamos."

I shook my head. "Riley is sure Sunshine Manor is a dummy corporation. That's why I need to see if anyone connected with Louisa Ralston has stayed there."

"Who says the person stayed there? Maybe someone just lifted the photo from the site."

"You've got a point. When I get to the shop, I'll run into the office and check. But if I'm right, and the photo taken from the back isn't available online, I'm going to Los Alamos."

"Even if you *are* right — and you probably are —" Mom said, "you don't have to shut down your shop and go there. Simply call the owners and give them a list of suspects."

"Okay. You're right. This is just the first solid lead I've run across as to who might've killed Louisa and Adam. What time does your flight leave?"

"Not until seven o'clock this evening. I'll make dinner."

"Let me take you out," I said.

She smiled. "Deal."

I retrieved Angus from the backyard, and he and I got into the Jeep and headed for the shop. Though it was cloudy, it wasn't rainy today, and I was glad of that. When I arrived at the shop, there was a car parked in my usual space. I parked beside it, and Angus and I got out. Eleanor Ralston got out of the other car.

"Marcy, good morning," she said. "I was waiting to talk with you."

"Come on in," I said, unlocking the shop door. I went inside and flipped on the lights. "Is anything wrong?"

"Oh, no," Eleanor said. "The opposite, really. I was at Adam Gray's office earlier helping Marsha — I'm going back there in a bit — and I wanted to thank you for being so kind to her. Mr. Gray was practically the only family she had."

"It's my pleasure." I didn't tell Eleanor I was mainly fishing for information, and her compliment about my kindness made me feel a twinge of guilt. "Have a seat. I'll put my jacket and purse in my office and be right with you."

I put my things in my office and took a rawhide chew for Angus out of his toy box. He stretched out on the floor with the treat, and I returned to the sit-and-stitch square.

"How long had you worked for Mr. Gray?" I asked Eleanor.

"I'm just finishing up paralegal training in a few weeks," she said, "but he was letting me work with him as a favor to Grandma. It was a great way to gain experience."

"What will you do now?"

"I'm applying for jobs in sunny California." Eleanor gave me a half smile. "I'm so tired of Oregon. Besides, I have nothing to keep me here now. The house is gone, the furnishings are gone. . . . I'm going to sublet my apartment and use the proceeds from the auction to start over in northern California."

"Good for you. I know all about starting

over," I said. "I left accounting in San Francisco to become an embroidery shop owner here in Tallulah Falls."

Eleanor chuckled. "Like Cary told you on Saturday, I was a nurse for a little while. It was a shame to throw away the education and the expense of nursing school. But after being in that field for three years, I couldn't do it anymore. It's exhausting — physically, mentally, emotionally." She sighed. "There was one patient in particular. Her name was Clarissa Simons. She was young. She appeared to be so full of life when I met her, but her body was riddled with cancer. I watched her deteriorate day after day until she died."

"I'm so sorry."

"It was then I decided life is too short to waste. The day she died was the day I gave up nursing."

"Wow," I said. "That's quite a story."

"It was quite an experience." She turned to me, seeming to shake off the melancholy of reminiscing about Clarissa Simons. "So, Marcy, do you know any attorneys in northern California who might be looking for a good paralegal?"

"I'll check with my mom's attorney and see," I said. "He has excellent connections."

"Thank you. I appreciate that." She stood.

"I'll be in town for at least another month, so if you come up with anything, please let me know."

I assured her I would, and she left. I returned to the office and booted up my computer. As soon as I had logged on to the Internet, I did a search for the Victorian Mansion at Los Alamos. As suspected, the photograph of the back of the building wasn't on the bed-and-breakfast's Web site. I couldn't find it on any of the other search sites, either. I copied down the B and B's phone number.

The photograph encompassed the mansion's large yard surrounded by the white picket fence — a perfect illustration for a brochure advertising a children's home. And whoever had taken it had been there.

I took out the *Boulevard of Broken Dreams* piece I was working on for Mom's birthday. Since she wouldn't be in today, I hoped I could get quite a bit of work done on it.

I returned to the sit-and-stitch square with the project, the phone number, and my cell phone. I punched in the number for the Victorian Mansion at Los Alamos, and then I put the phone on speaker and waited for someone to answer. Since the project was stamped on the fabric, I was able to stitch without worrying about counting, which made multitasking much easier.

"Good morning, the Victorian Mansion at Los Alamos," a cheerful voice answered.

"Good morning. My name is Marcy Singer, and I'm calling from Tallulah Falls, Oregon. My mother and I stayed in your Egyptian Room several years ago."

"And you're calling to reserve the room again?" she asked.

"No, I'm afraid not. I believe someone used a photograph of the Victorian Mansion in a brochure for a nonexistent children's home called Sunshine Manor."

"Are you certain it's our bed-and-breakfast?" she asked.

"I'll be happy to fax you the brochure, and you can see for yourself," I said.

"Would you?"

"Of course. I know this is a long shot, but the reason I'm calling is to ask you to go back through your records of the past couple years to see if any of the people suspected in defrauding this lady stayed at your bed-and-breakfast."

"I guess I could do that," she said. "Are you a police officer or federal agent or —"

"Um . . . actually, I'm. . . ."

At that moment, Ted Nash walked through the door. I held up the phone to let him know I was on speaker.

"Actually," I said, "I'm with Chief Detective Ted Nash of the Tallulah Falls Police Department."

"All right," the woman said. "If you'll fax me the brochure and the list of names, I'll look into this matter right away."

"Thank you so much for your help," I said.

I ended the call and smiled at Ted. "Hello."

"Why do I get the feeling I'm being punked or something?" he asked. "I come in, and you're on the phone and you suddenly tell the person on the other end, *I'm with Ted Nash.*"

I bit my lip. "Well, I needed her help and I . . . kinda thought it would sound better coming from you."

"You thought what would sound better coming from me?"

I explained about Sunshine Manor, the brochure, and the Victorian Mansion at Los Alamos. Then I backtracked and told Ted about Mom and me going to the historical society and learning about Louisa's baby by Edward Larkin. "Mom, Riley, and I were able to find out that Louisa had a baby named Ivy while she was at Tipton-Haney House. The baby was adopted by a couple with the surname Sutherland."

"Having a child in a women's home like

that would make Louisa open to supporting a similar charity," Ted said.

"Right. And whoever set her up knew that. I believe that if the woman at the Victorian Mansion at Los Alamos can look back through her guest records and find a person connected to Louisa Ralston, then we have our fraud agent *and* we just might have Mrs. Ralston's killer."

"Excellent work, Inch-High Private Eye." He grinned.

"Thanks," I said, ignoring the jibe. "But get this — according to Marsha, Adam Gray's secretary, Ms. Ellis is the one who told Louisa Ralston about Sunshine Manor."

"Then you believe Ms. Ellis is involved?" Ted asked.

"Not directly, but I think someone connected to her might be."

"You mean Cary."

I closed my eyes. "I don't want it to be, but . . . yeah, I think it might be."

"Have you spoken with Ms. Ellis?" he asked.

"No. What would I do? Call her up and asked how she found out about Sunshine Manor?"

"I'll feed this lead to Detectives Ray and

Bailey," he said. "They'll follow up with Ms. Ellis."

"You don't think they'll be too hard on her, do you?"

He shook his head. "They're tough, but they're not abusive. Even if she is the person who did her sister in, they'll handle her with kid gloves."

"Wait. You don't think that's possible, do you?" I asked.

"In this business, I've learned *anything* is possible." He began ticking off items on his fingers. "She suggested Sunshine Manor. She takes Halumet. She may have been resentful of Louisa."

"But, Ted, Ms. Ellis has all that money! She has that gigantic house and —"

"It's not always about money," he said. "Sometimes there are factors far more volatile. I have a cousin who is a marshal in Savannah. He says the saying there is, *In the South, you only kill those you really, really love.*"

"I've seen my share of detective shows." I set the stitchery project aside. "Nine times out of ten, it *is* about the money."

He wrinkled his brow. "I'd say seven times out of ten. But the other three times, it has something to do with love."

"So who all do you think I should put on

the list of people who had it in for Mrs. Ralston?" I asked.

"Millicent Ellis, Cary Ellis, Frank Ralston —"

"Frank? Why? Hasn't he been dead too long to be involved?"

"He has," Ted agreed, "but someone might've used his name at the B and B. In fact, go ahead and put Louisa Ralston's name on that list, too."

"All right. Who else?"

He sighed. "Adam Gray, Marsha . . . whatever her last name is, Eleanor Ralston, Edward Larkin, Ivy Larkin, Ivy Sutherland. And you."

"Me?"

He nodded. "Don't forget, there might be a reason Louisa Ralston collapsed here in your shop rather than someplace else."

# CHAPTER TWENTY-FIVE

I was sitting on one of the red chairs in the sit-and-stitch square working on Mom's birthday present when Sadie came in after the lunch rush.

"I looked around this morning, and you'd gone," she said, coming over to sit on the sofa facing away from the window.

I nodded. "It was obvious you were upset with me, and I didn't want to deal with that. So I got my cappuccinos and muffins at the coffeehouse near Adam Gray's office."

"Sorry about that." She leaned back into the sofa cushions. "I was just feeling weird. This weekend I began second-guessing things all over again. Whether I could really trust Blake . . . whether or not he truly loves me . . . whether anyone's relationship actually winds up 'happily ever after.' "

"Sadie, you've got to quit doing that. You told me yourself that you were following the steps to regaining trust, and one of those steps was to make the conscious effort to trust."

"I know. I love Blake with all my heart, and I'm terrified of getting hurt." She sighed. "I know his breach of trust wasn't life-shattering — it's not like he had an affair or anything — but it still scares me."

"He adores you. Trust him."

"You're right. I know you're right. So what about you and Todd . . . and you and Ted?" she asked.

"Whatever is meant to be will be," I said, stitching the diner's counter in the *Boulevard of Broken Dreams.* "I'm not rushing into anything with either one. But I've been hurt so badly in the past . . . and I think both Todd and Ted have, too. We all need to know where we're going and what we want before any of us try to pursue a relationship. You know what I mean?"

"Yeah, I do. I got lucky. Blake was my first real love . . . and he still is."

I smiled. "You *did* get lucky."

"Did I tell you we're trying for a baby again?" she asked. "I think that's why I'm feeling panicky and afraid to trust again. That's such a huge step."

"I know. But I also know you two will make terrific parents." I tilted my head. "Plus, Riley has given me lots of practice making bibs and other baby things, so I'll be ready when you do get pregnant."

She stood. "I'd better get back over to the café before Blake gets swamped."

As she was leaving, my phone rang.

"Hi, Ms. Singer," the perky female voice said. "This is Debbie with the Victorian Mansion in Los Alamos. I've had a chance to look over your fax."

"And?" *Sorry, but I was impatient.*

"You're right about the house on the brochure. It isn't Sunshine Manor. It's the back entrance to the Victorian Mansion. But none of the people on your list has ever stayed here . . . unless they did so under another name."

"You're sure?" I asked.

"Double-checked. Is there anyone else you'd like me to look for?"

"No, but thank you so much."

"Call me back if you need anything else," she said. "I'm not particularly crazy about a photo of our bed-and-breakfast being used to scam people, either."

That evening I took Mom to the seafood restaurant overlooking the ocean that Cary had taken us to. She ordered salmon steak this time, and I ordered tilapia.

"The bed-and-breakfast lead was a bust,"

I said, as I tore open a garlic cheese biscuit.

"Really?"

I nodded. "The woman said none of the names on my list came up. On Ted's advice, I even added my name to the list."

She frowned. "And, of course, your name would've never come up because when we stayed there it was under my name."

"Right. So if our Sunshine Manor person stayed with someone else, then we'll never know."

Mom reached across the table and patted my hand. "It'll all work out. You'll see."

"I know." Actually, I didn't know. I didn't have a clue. But I didn't want her to worry more than she was already.

"What a surprise!"

I looked up to see Devon Reed and Ella Redmond standing by our table. It was Devon who'd spoken.

"Hello," I said wearily.

"Did you enjoy yourselves at the auction?" Mom asked archly.

"Supremely," Devon said.

"I did, too," Ella said. "I bought the portrait of Louisa Ralston."

My eyes widened. "You bought the portrait? I can't believe Eleanor included that in the auction."

"Yes, well, it's a lovely portrait, and I have

a vacant wall in my living room." She smiled. "It looks beautiful. You'll have to come by and see it."

"Yes, I will," I said.

"Why did you buy a portrait of someone you didn't know?" Mom asked.

"I don't know," Ella said. "I felt sad for her, I suppose."

"Besides, it'll look great in the documentary," said Devon, "if we're able to find out what happened to Mrs. Ralston."

"Yes," I said, "I guess it will."

Devon glanced at the maître d', who'd been leading them to their table. "We need to get to our table and stop holding this man up. We'll talk with you soon."

"Take care," I said.

Mom shook her head. "Those two are strange ones. I guess they make a good couple after all."

I merely rolled my eyes and dug into my tilapia again. We needed to finish our dinner and get to the airport.

That evening while Angus wrestled a rubber bone filled with peanut butter up and down the hallway, I sat propped up in the bed with my laptop, trying to find out what had happened to Ivy Sutherland. I logged on to a genealogy site and did a search for

*Ivy Sutherland of Kansas.* After nearly an hour of searching, I found a woman named Ivy Sutherland who had married a man by the name of Halstead. Ivy's husband was listed as Baker . . . not his profession, but his name. Baker Halstead. That was an unusual name.

Ivy and Baker Halstead had two children, Ella Louise Halstead and Devon Reed Halstead.

My heart suddenly began trying to beat its way out of my chest. Ella and Devon were Louisa Ralston's grandchildren? Could that actually be true? And if it was true, could Ella and Devon have orchestrated Louisa's death in order to get what they felt their mother had deserved all along?

I grabbed the phone and dialed Ella's cell phone number.

"Hello," she answered in an almost tentative voice.

"Ella, it's Marcy Singer."

"Is anything wrong?" she asked. "You sound upset."

"Why didn't you tell me you were Louisa Ralston's granddaughter?"

There was a click, and the phone went dead. I immediately tried to call back, but the call went directly to voice mail. I was sitting there debating on whether to call Riley or Ted or to gather more information about Ella and Devon. I decided to gather information first. After all, I didn't have very much time left on the site's free trial period.

Ella had been married to John Redmond, but they had divorced. Devon had not been married as far as I could tell. There was a death record for Baker Halstead, but I was unable to find one for Ivy Halstead.

When the doorbell rang, I instinctively glanced at the clock, and Angus began barking. It was after nine o'clock. Grateful that I hadn't gotten ready for bed yet, I slipped on my shoes and went downstairs to open the door. Angus was right on my heels. I peeped through the keyhole to see Ella and Devon standing on the front porch. I opened the door.

"I'm sorry I hung up on you," Ella said. "I simply couldn't try to explain things to you over the phone. And I wanted Devon to be with me when we spoke to you."

Devon nodded. "Hello again."

"Hi." I stood back and hesitantly invited them in. I normally would've put Angus in the backyard, but I didn't this time. I was probably the only person in Tallulah Falls who knew Ella and Devon were Louisa's grandchildren. I wished I'd called Ted or Riley as I'd originally thought of doing.

Then at least if Ella and Devon killed me, someone would have known the truth.

Ella, Devon, and I walked into the living room. I sat on the chair, and they sat side by side on the sofa. Angus came to lie by my feet.

"Where do we start?" Ella asked her brother.

He shrugged. "I can start." He turned to me. "We didn't know our mom was Louisa Ralston's daughter until after Louisa Ralston was dead. We suspected, but we weren't sure."

"Why didn't you talk with Mrs. Ralston?" I asked.

"We wanted to be sure," Ella said. "That's not something you merely spring on someone because you think she *might* be your grandmother, especially when she's wealthy."

"Yeah," said Devon, "she probably had so-called relatives crawling out of the woodwork. We'd look like any other gold diggers if we didn't have proof that she was our biological grandmother."

"I'd been searching for Momma's birth mother for several months," Ella said. "And my search finally led me to Tipton-Haney House. The Sutherlands — although we loved them very much — hadn't been forthcoming with information about the adoption. All we knew was that Momma had been born in Oregon."

"When Mrs. Ralston died in your store," Devon said, "Ella called me."

"I was scared, Marcy. I thought people might think I'd had something to do with her murder."

I nodded. "I understand that. But why didn't you tell *me?*"

"I was still so new to Tallulah Falls," Ella said, "I didn't know who I could really trust. And I knew that if I began telling people I was Louisa Ralston's granddaughter, they'd think I was either lying or trying to cash in on her estate."

"And despite what you think of me," Devon said, "that's not what we're trying to do."

"Not at all," Ella said. "We just wanted to know her. I felt like I knew her already because I'd read so much about her. My heart ached for her when I realized how she'd been done by Edward Larkin."

"Did you find him?" I asked.

Ella nodded. "He died in a work-related accident in the fifties. He was in construction, and he fell off a scaffold."

"I'm sorry," I said. "Why did you go to such lengths to deceive me, Devon?"

Devon looked sheepish. "I wasn't as deceptive as you probably think. I really am a journalist, and I was at the prison attempting to talk with the businessman I told you about. It was just a fluke that I ran into you and your mother there."

"I wish you guys had been honest with me from the beginning," I said. "Is your mother still living? Do you realize she is entitled to a trust fund Mrs. Ralston set up for her several years ago?"

Ella nodded. "Yeah, Mom is living, but she has terminal cancer. She's in a hospice house at home in Kansas." Her eyes welled with tears, and Devon put his arm around her shoulders.

"We wanted to do this for her," he said. "We wanted her to be able to make contact with the mother she never knew."

"And the really terrible thing," Ella said, sniffling, "is that Mrs. Ralston wanted that, too. She'd actually been looking for Momma until the day *she* died."

I ran my hands down my face. "You have to come forward, guys. You have to."

"It doesn't matter now," Ella said. "All that really matters is finding out who killed our grandmother and why."

"I think I know the why," I said. I explained to them about Sunshine Manor and the fraudulent children's home. "If your mother doesn't come forward to claim that trust fund, the money will revert to Sunshine Manor, and whoever killed her will get the money he or she was after."

Ella sighed and looked at her brother. "What do you think?"

A muscle worked in his jaw while he considered what to do about the situation. "I don't want whoever killed our grandmother to profit from her death and get away scot-free." Suddenly his face brightened. "Revealing ourselves to the world might be the perfect way to draw out the killer hiding behind Sunshine Manor."

# Chapter Twenty-Six

I called Riley and put the phone on speaker. I apologized for calling so late, but when I explained what was going on, she was glad I had.

"The commission from this case might cover Baby Kendall's first year or two of college," she said with a laugh.

Riley agreed to represent the Halstead siblings in their attempt to claim Ivy League's trust fund. She didn't think there would be much trouble getting the trust fund, even without their mother present for any legal proceedings — Ella already had her mother's power of attorney, due to her health. But like Ella and me, Riley was worried about the repercussions of ticking off Mrs. Ralston's killer. Devon seemed gung ho to have the killer "bring it."

"Have you fully thought this out, Ella and Devon?" Riley asked. "This person has already killed twice for this money. I'm guessing that racking up two more bodies won't weigh too heavily on his or her conscience."

"It's a risk we're willing to take," Devon said.

"I'm going to call Ted Nash as soon as we hang up," I said. "He'll be able to advise us about security measures and might even be able to offer some help in that area."

"That's great, Marce," Riley said, "but don't go completely renegade with regard to the Tallulah County cops. They don't need to be blindsided with this. Even if they tell you it's stupid, advise them of what we're doing."

"What *are* we doing?" Ella asked.

"You'll come into my office tomorrow morning first thing. I don't have any appointments until after lunch. Bring your proof of identity and claims to Mrs. Ralston's estate. I'll need to schedule DNA testing. Does either of you have a problem with that?"

Both Ella and Devon said they did not.

"It would be better to test Mrs. Ralston's DNA against your mother's DNA," Riley said, "but yours might be a close enough match. We're going to announce that in a press conference at around eleven thirty tomorrow morning. I'll have my mom —

er, my secretary — send out an event release first thing tomorrow. The two of you need to be with me at my office as I announce to the press that long-lost relatives of Louisa Ralston have come forward to claim a trust fund Mrs. Ralston left to their mother. I'll say that DNA tests are being conducted but that we are confident, based on the evidence we have, that everything will go forward and that these siblings will inherit from the grandmother they never knew."

"There's your personal-interest piece, Devon," I said. I kind of regretted it as soon as I said it, but I figured he'd had it coming for quite a while.

Riley laughed. "Oh, it'll be a personal-interest piece, all right. You'll get your fill of reporters and gossipmongers. We'll take no questions but promise to keep the media informed as the story develops. Then we'll call an end to the press conference, I will return to my office, and the two of you can exit out the back."

"I'm a little scared," Ella said. "Whoever killed our grandmother and Mr. Gray is going to be gunning for us."

"But that's the point, El," Devon said. "We'll draw that person out. No way are we gonna let ourselves be poisoned. We'll be on our guard. It'll be okay."

"As your attorney, I must advise there is some risk involved here," Riley said. "Ella, you are absolutely correct in that you'll be bait to draw out this killer. And just because poison has been the weapon of choice in the deaths of Louisa and Adam doesn't mean he or she doesn't have a gun or won't try to run you over with a car or whatever. If you're having second thoughts, tell me and I'll ditch the press conference."

"No," Ella said, taking a deep, steadying breath. "I want to do this."

After we spoke to Riley, I called Ted.

"Ted Nash," he answered in his professional, no-nonsense detective voice.

"Hi," I said. "It's Marcy . . . and you're on speaker."

He chuckled. "Why am I dreading this conversation before it even begins? Who else am I talking with?"

"Ella Redmond and Devon Reed," I said.

"This ought to be good," he said.

Ella, Devon, and I explained everything to Ted. It was a jumbled mess at times with us talking over one another, but we got the main points across. Devon and Ella were Louisa Ralston's grandchildren; they stood to inherit the trust fund Mrs. Ralston had set aside for Ivy; and they and Riley were going to hold a press conference tomorrow to make sure Mrs. Ralston's killer knew all this.

When we finished, Ted was silent.

"Are you there, Ted?" I asked.

"I'm afraid so," he answered.

"You aren't going to try to talk us out of this, are you?" I asked.

"Would there be any point?" He heaved a breath. "All right. Here's how we're going to do this. I'm going to get in touch with Detectives Bailey and Ray of the Tallulah County Police Department as soon as their shift starts tomorrow morning and prepare them for that interview. I'll put in a request for extra security on all of you. Devon, stay put."

"Stay put where?" Devon asked.

"Preferably with Ella to conserve manpower," Ted said. "I'll ask the TCPD to put some men on you, too."

"What about Riley?" I asked.

"Her, too," he said. "We have to be sure to cover all our bases when dealing with this nutcase."

That night before I turned in, I phoned Mom and told her the latest. Then I called Angus and had him get up on the bed beside me. Plotting to bring a killer out into the open makes a girl want an enormous dog by her side.

■ ■ ■ ■

It didn't take long after the press conference for the repercussions to start. Sadie was the first to pop into the Seven-Year Stitch.

"Do you believe it?" she asked. "Blake and I just saw on one of the TVs we have on at the café that Ella Redmond and Devon Reed are brother and sister and that they're Louisa Ralston's grandchildren." Slack-jawed, she flopped onto the sofa. "Unreal. Riley Kendall called a press conference and announced it a few minutes ago."

I was working on Mom's birthday present — the *Boulevard of Broken Dreams* piece — and barely looked up. "Really?"

"That's not an I'm-so-shocked *really,*" Sadie said. "You already knew, didn't you?"

I told her what had transpired the night before and swore her to secrecy.

"Do you think they truly are Louisa Ralston's grandchildren or that this is merely another scam?" she asked.

"The DNA test will tell us for certain."

The next person to come in — regarding the press conference rather than seeking embroidery supplies — was Eleanor Ralston. She stormed into the shop looking wild-eyed and shaken.

"Did you see the press conference?" she asked.

"No," I said. And that was the truth. I didn't have a TV in the shop. "What press conference?"

"That idiot reporter and some woman who works at the library have come forward to say that my grandmother had an illegitimate child when she was young and that the child grew up to become their mother." Eleanor paced and gesticulated frantically as she spoke. "Can you imagine? They only want money, and they're dragging my grandmother's name through the mud to get it." She whirled and pointed at me. "I'm schooled in law, you know. And I will prevent this from going any further. They will *not* sully the Ralston name, and they will *not* get a cent from our family. In fact, I'm thinking of suing them for slander." She snatched a tissue from the box on the counter and held it to her nose. "I'm sorry, Marcy. I shouldn't unload on you like this."

"It's all right," I said. "I understand."

"This whole thing is because Grandma came into this store looking for ivy . . . ivy-colored thread, more than likely. And since their mother's name is Ivy, they think they have something to tie them to our family.

But they don't." She pitched the tissue into the wastebasket and took another. "They can't do this. It was never even proven that Grandma had a child at Tipton-Haney House. She volunteered there because she cared so much about children. That's all."

I nodded.

"She *was* looking for ivy-colored thread when she came in here, wasn't she?" Eleanor asked. "You'll testify to that, won't you?"

"I'll . . . I'll say exactly what she said to me," I said.

Eleanor smiled. "Thank you." She turned and left.

I waved good-bye, thinking she wouldn't be thanking me if she did, in fact, call me to testify about what Mrs. Ralston had said. The woman never once mentioned thread.

Eleanor wasn't the only Ralston relation who visited the Seven-Year Itch that day. Cary, too, paid a visit.

"Hi," I said, a bit nervously. Was he here because he thought I had played a part in the Ella-and-Devon sideshow? After all, it was his mother who had suggested that Louisa donate her money to Sunshine Manor. "Didn't Mom call you yesterday?"

"She did," he said. "I trust she had a safe flight home?"

"Yes. I spoke with her last night."

He smiled. "Good." He put his hands in his pockets and rocked back and forth on his heels. "That was a surprising press conference today, wasn't it?"

"I didn't see it myself," I said, "but Eleanor was here earlier, and she was talking about it."

"Was she upset?" he asked.

"Yes. She was downright furious, saying that the Halsteads are intending to drag the Ralston name through the mud," I said.

He nodded. "Mother is, too."

I wondered if his mother was worried about the Ralston name being dragged through the mud or about losing the money earmarked for Sunshine Manor.

"Eleanor said she doesn't believe Louisa had a child while she was working at Tipton-Haney House . . . that she was only there as a volunteer," I said. "What does your mother think?"

He gazed up at the ceiling. "I believe Mother knows the truth, but she doesn't want to admit it."

"Then you think she did have a child and that Devon and Ella could be that child's progeny?" I asked.

"It's possible." He gave me a tight smile. "We'll have to wait and see, won't we?"

"I guess so."

He took a business card from his pocket and handed it to me. "I know you have classes for the next three evenings — I'll be here tonight, of course — but your mom bought you a dress at my boutique."

"She what?"

He chuckled. "It was to be a surprise . . . so, surprise!"

I frowned. "I don't understand."

"Beverly wanted to buy you a dress, but since you couldn't get away, and since you've been under so much stress, she wanted you to have it after she'd gone. She said you could wear it on a date with one of your young men." He winked. "Maybe on Friday afternoon after you close the shop, you can come by and get the dress?"

"What does it look like?" I asked.

He laughed again. "That's the beauty of it. You get to pick it out yourself. So come — the boutique will be at your disposal."

"Thank you," I said. "I really appreciate this."

"Thank your mother," he said. "It's her gift. See you later on. You'll be surprised at how well my lion is coming along."

Things picked up not long after Cary was in, and I didn't have time to call Mom and thank her for the dress. I didn't have time to work on her cross-stitch project, either. I sold embroidery needles, canvases, and more white yarn.

The last person to enter the shop solely to talk about the morning's press conference was Marsha, Adam Gray's secretary. She came in just before I closed up for dinner.

"Nice shop," she said. "I like the mannequin."

"Thank you."

"Were you getting ready to leave?" she asked.

"No, that's okay. I have class here tonight, and although I usually close up and go home for dinner and to put Angus in the backyard, I sometimes just grab a bite to eat at MacKenzies' Mochas . . . especially when I leave Angus at home with a bowl of food like I did today." I smiled. "Whenever we have a nice day, I like to let him stay home and play in the yard. What can I help you with?"

"Oh, I don't do embroidery," Marsha said. "I wish I could, but I'm not very good at things like that. I came about Riley's press conference this morning. Do you think those people are who they say they are?"

"I don't know, Marsha. I guess we'll have to wait for the DNA tests to tell us."

"Yeah . . . I guess so. Do you think they

killed Mrs. Ralston and Adam in order to get that trust fund?"

"No," I said. "I think — I hope — they really wanted to know their grandmother. What do you think?"

She shrugged.

"I mean, what would they gain by killing her?" I asked. "All they'd have had to do is go to Mrs. Ralston and present their case. That would've solved everything, and no one would've got hurt. Right?"

She shrugged again. "Not if they're frauds."

I hadn't considered that.

# Chapter Twenty-Seven

We had a full house for class that evening. Cary was there. Reggie Singh, Vera Langhorne, Ella, and Devon were there, too. Devon was there because Ted had instructed him to stay with Ella. He was sticking to his sister like glue.

The only one missing from the stitchers was Sadie. One of her waitresses had called in sick, and she didn't want to leave Blake shorthanded.

"Devon," I asked, after everyone else got to work on their projects, "would you like to try your hand at needlepoint?"

"No, thanks," he said. "I'm doing fine reading this *GQ*."

"All right," I said. "But if you get bored, just say so."

Despite the full class and one extra person, an awkward silence filled the sit-and-stitch square. Cary was avoiding eye contact with Ella and Devon. Ella was avoiding eye contact with everyone except me. Devon was hiding behind his magazine. And Vera was bursting to talk about the press conference but knew that to do so would be a huge social faux pas. We could literally hear the clock on the far wall ticking as we worked. I attempted to make small talk a time or two, but I finally gave up.

Ten minutes or so before the end of class, everyone started putting their materials away.

"That was fun," Vera said, as she left. "See you tomorrow, Marcy."

"Don't forget about Friday," Cary said, filing out the door.

Eventually, the only people left were Devon, Ella, and me. I smiled at them. "How did it go today?"

"I think it went all right," Ella said. "Riley knew what she was talking about with the reporters and gossipmongers. They hounded us for a while, but they finally gave us some peace when we said we'd let the media know as soon as the DNA results come back."

"The shop was abuzz with talk of the press conference, too," I said.

"Is that what you wanted us to stay after class to discuss?" Devon asked.

I frowned. "If you want to, we can."

"Didn't you e-mail me at the library and ask us to plan to stay for a few minutes after class because you had something to talk with us about?" Ella asked.

I slowly shook my head. "Guys, I think we've been set up. We need to get out of here. Let's go out the back way."

I felt a burst of cold air and turned.

Eleanor was standing in the open doorway of the shop. "No, please don't leave. I'm the one who sent the e-mail." She stepped in, setting the bells above her head to jingling. "I wanted the four of us to be able to talk somewhere privately." She moved into the sit-and-stitch square and sat down on the sofa beside Ella. "I'm sorry about your mother. I knew someone who had terminal cancer, and I know how horrible it is."

"Yes, it is," Ella said.

"And I realize you want your mother to have the very best treatment," Eleanor continued. "I have money. If you'll please drop all this nonsense about my grandmother having a child out of wedlock, I'll see to it that your mother is well cared for in her final days."

"It isn't nonsense," Devon said. "Ivy Larkin Sutherland Halstead is our mother. And she was born to Louisa Ralston in nineteen forty-three at Tipton-Haney House."

"You're grasping at straws," Eleanor said. "I've seen those records. The children were dubbed *Baby So-and-So,* and their parents weren't mentioned in the records."

"Unofficially, yes," Ella said. "But they had birth records. And those birth records listed both the mother and the father — when known — of the child. Our mother's original birth certificate listed her mother as Louisa Ralston and her father as Edward Larkin."

"Baby Ivy born at Tipton-Haney House in nineteen forty-three has a birth certificate listing Mildred and Arthur Sutherland as her parents," Eleanor said.

"That was the birth certificate granted to the Sutherlands after they adopted Momma," Ella said. "The first certificate contained the names of her biological parents."

"Here's what I can't figure out," I said. "Riley and I went online, and Mom and I visited the Tallulah Falls Historical Society, and we found out about Ivy's parentage within a matter of hours. How is it that Ella and Mrs. Ralston were unable to connect?"

"I only began searching when Momma was diagnosed with cancer," Ella said. "I wanted to reunite her with her biological parents, if possible."

"I was doing the searching for Grandma," Eleanor said, finally dropping all pretenses that she didn't believe Ivy to be Louisa's daughter, "and it was my intention that she never find the illegitimate child of Edward Larkin."

"It wasn't your call to make," Devon said. "She was our grandmother, and we had a right to know her. She had a right to know us and our mother."

"It was my call to make," Eleanor said, "because she was *my* grandmother. I'm the one who cared for her, ran her errands, paid her bills, and cleaned her house because she was too proud to hire help. I'm the one who deserved to get the money she left in that stupid trust fund for a daughter she'd given away nearly seven decades ago. Grandma never found Ivy Larkin because I never looked for her."

"What about Adam Gray?" I asked. "Didn't he know about Ivy Larkin?"

"Who knows?" Eleanor asked. "Who cares?" She glared at Devon and Ella. "That money is mine. Once again, I'll be happy to throw a little your way, but you're not getting that entire trust fund."

I noticed Eleanor slipping her hand into the pocket of her coat. "That sounds reasonable," I said, looking pointedly at Ella and

Devon. "Don't you guys think it is? Maybe Eleanor can provide a little money for your mom to help her be more comfortable, and you guys can cancel the DNA test and say everything was a mistake."

Devon wasn't given to subtlety and wouldn't have known a hint had it slapped him across the face. "No way. If Louisa Ralston wanted our mother to have that money, then she's going to get it." He looked at Eleanor. "You got the house and the furniture and all the rest. That should be enough for you to do well on."

Eleanor's hand slid deeper into her pocket.

Ella saw my ever-widening eyes and caught on. "No, Devon. Marcy's right. We should accept Eleanor's generous offer and drop this thing. We don't want to embarrass our late grandmother, do we?"

Eleanor shook her head. "He won't drop it. He's too greedy." She withdrew a small pistol from her coat pocket. "It's not fair. I deserve that money. I deserve everything."

"Please, Eleanor," I said. "Think about what you're doing. This situation doesn't have to play out like this."

"Yeah, I think it does." She stood, pointing the pistol at Devon as she moved to a corner of the sit-and-stitch square where she could keep an eye on all of us but have her back to the window.

Suddenly Ted, Detective Bailey, and Detective Ray burst into the shop. Someone yelled, "Drop the gun!" I thought it was Ted, but I wasn't sure. Everything happened so fast. Eleanor did drop the gun. Detective Ray handcuffed her, and Detective Bailey began reciting her rights.

Ted hugged me while Devon and Ella hugged each other. I clung to Ted as tightly as my trembling arms would allow.

"It's okay," he said. "It's over."

"A-are you sure? How did you know to come here? What . . . ?" My knees started to give way.

He gently picked me up and moved me over to the sofa as Detectives Bailey and Ray left with Eleanor. "We — the Tallulah County detectives and I — had someone watching all the Ralstons, plus Riley, the Halsteads, and you." He kissed my forehead. "I was actually watching you."

"Manu didn't mind?"

"I called him last night and took a vacation day. I knew something major would go down after that press conference, and I know you well enough to realize you'd be right in the middle of it."

"How did you know it was Eleanor?" I asked.

"We didn't. Detective Ray was following her. It seemed awfully convenient when she arrived and you and Ella and Devon were the only people still here."

"She had to know that if she shot us, she'd go to prison and not get anything."

"She'll be going to prison. After this fiasco, it won't be hard to connect the dots," Ted said.

Ella and Devon came to sit on the other sofa so they could hear Ted's explanation.

"Eleanor has nurse's training," he continued, "and she used to care for Ms. Ellis, who takes Halumet. Also, if Ms. Ellis trusted Eleanor, it would be easy for Eleanor to put the suggestion of Sunshine Manor into her head."

"I see what you're saying," I said. "Ms. Ellis knew of her sister's love of children. Eleanor could have brought the brochure by and mentioned it to Ms. Ellis as a company that was dedicated to finding good homes for orphaned children."

"She could've even played up the orphanage's need for funding," Devon said. "That's how I'd have done it."

"You would not have convinced an old woman to have her sister buy into a dummy corporation," Ella scolded.

"Probably not," he agreed, "but I can see

how Eleanor could've gone about it."

"I wonder how Eleanor got both Louisa and Adam to ingest the Halumet," I said.

"That wouldn't be hard," Ted said. "I'm told Halumet doesn't have much of a flavor but that it is a little bitter. It could have easily been dissolved and concealed in a cup of coffee."

I released a deflated breath. "I'm so glad this mess is over."

"Me, too," Ella said. "Devon, did you talk with the detectives? Can we go?"

"Yeah," Devon said. "The detectives said they'll take each of our statements tomorrow morning."

"Need a ride home?" Ted asked me.

"Thank you. A ride home would be great."

# Epilogue

On a hunch the next day, I called the Victorian Mansion at Los Alamos and asked if a Clarissa Simons had ever stayed there. A quick check of their records showed that Ms. Simons had stayed at the bed-and-breakfast on more than one occasion. I told them I believed that was an alias for Eleanor Ralston and that she was the one who'd used the photograph of the bed-and-breakfast for the Sunshine Manor brochure.

DNA evidence proved that Devon and Ella were indeed Louisa Ralston's grandchildren, and Devon wound up giving me the umbrella stand for my help in bringing his grandmother's killer to justice. It's now standing in the corner of the Seven-Year Stitch, and we're having an unusual dry spell. Figures.

I was able to finish the *Boulevard of Broken Dreams* cross-stitch picture just in time for Mom's birthday. She adored it. When I went to California to celebrate with her, I wore the dress she'd bought me from Cary's boutique. It was a wine-colored silk wrap dress with trumpet sleeves. It was stunning.

Frances had thrown Mom a small celebration with a delicious dinner and a lovely cake. Cary had sent flowers.

After all the guests had left, I went over to smell the bouquet of red roses he'd had delivered. "The man has class," I said, with a smile. "I'm so glad he wasn't the killer. I had my doubts there a time or two."

"I didn't," Mom said. "I told you, Cary Grant never played a villain."

The employees of Thorndike Press hope you have enjoyed this Large Print book. All our Thorndike, Wheeler, and Kennebec Large Print titles are designed for easy reading, and all our books are made to last. Other Thorndike Press Large Print books are available at your library, through selected bookstores, or directly from us.

For information about titles, please call:
(800) 223-1244

or visit our Web site at:
http://gale.cengage.com/thorndike

To share your comments, please write:
Publisher
Thorndike Press
10 Water St., Suite 310
Waterville, ME 04901

3 2953 01108067 0